"You Have A Mr. Right Checklist?"

It made him uncomfortably aware that she was weighing everything he did and said. He needed to watch himself around her.

Gail shrugged. "It's just qualities I think would be compatible with me. Like, I'm looking for someone with a good job."

"Check that one off for me."

She smiled at him. "And he has to be committed to the person he's dating."

"Ah. That one will be harder to convince you of, won't it?"

"Yes. You aren't exactly known for monogamy. And then…" She hesitated as a pretty pink blush spread up to her cheeks.

"What could be next?" he asked. "Why are you so shy now?"

"I have to be attracted to you. A healthy sex life is on my checklist."

He leaned in close, his breath hot on her neck. "When the time is right you will have no doubts that I can fulfill all your needs."

Dear Reader,

My new series from Harlequin Desire is kicking off with a juicy, scandal-ridden romance! Russell Holloway was a secondary character in my Miami Nights miniseries so you might remember him from there. In this book he meets his match in Gail Little, who is Russell's antithesis. Where he's a free spirit whose escapades are always heralded on the internet, she's staid and quiet and looking for Mr. Right.

Some matchmaker thinks Russell might be that guy, but PR guru Gail thinks it might be a setup to clean up Russell's image. Russell starts out with ulterior motives but soon finds himself falling for Gail. He never would have thought that Ms. Right would be so classy, so refined and so damned sexy!

I hope you enjoy the start to this new series.

Happy reading!

Katherine

KATHERINE GARBERA

READY FOR HER CLOSE-UP

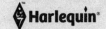

Desire

Recycling programs
for this product may
not exist in your area.

ISBN-13: 978-0-373-73173-2

READY FOR HER CLOSE-UP

This edition published by arrangement with Harlequin Books S.A.

For questions and comments about the quality of this book please contact us at Customer_eCare@Harlequin.ca.

® and TM are trademarks of Harlequin Books S.A., used under license. Trademarks indicated with ® are registered in the United States Patent and Trademark Office, the Canadian Trade Marks Office and in other countries.

www.Harlequin.com

Printed in U.S.A.

Books by Katherine Garbera

Harlequin Desire

KATHERINE GARBERA

is a *USA TODAY* bestselling author of more than forty books who has always believed in happy endings. She lives in England with her husband, children and their pampered pet, Godiva. Visit Katherine on the web at www.katherinegarbera.com, or catch up with her on Facebook and Twitter.

This one is for my family for always believing in me and making me feel special even though I know I'm not.

One

What had she been thinking?

Gail Little took a deep breath and walked into the makeshift hair and makeup area for the set of the reality-TV dating show *Sexy and Single*. She had never in her entire life thought of herself as sexy, but single…now, that was something she had buttoned up. She'd always thought she'd hook up with a guy in college, and they'd fall into a relationship as they both started their careers. Then, after three years of dating, they'd get married, but now she was staring down thirty and still alone.

"I'm Kat Humphries, the PA for *Sexy and Single*. I'll also be your handler for all of your segments."

Gail shook Kat's hand. She'd expected to see Willow Stead—the producer of the show and one of her best friends—instead of a PA. Willow had gotten the idea to do the show when Gail had signed up with Matchmakers Inc. Though Gail had only told her friends she wanted to find a husband and didn't meet the right kind of men at work, the truth was she wanted a family of her own and her biological clock was ticking. So she'd signed on with the dating service, never expecting her experiences would become the focus of a TV show.

Kat looked to be in her mid-twenties and wore a pair of slim-fitting jeans and a T-shirt from a bar in Mexico. Her long brown hair was pulled back in a ponytail, and she had an earpiece attached to the radio at her belt.

"Follow me," Kat said.

Gail nodded and went with her to a bank of lighted mirrors set up against the wall. This was behind-the-scenes television that few viewers ever saw. Not very glamorous, but as the owner of a very successful PR firm, it was a world Gail knew well. Funny that she never pictured herself as the one going onstage.

"Have a seat here. The hair and makeup people are on their way. You're a few minutes early."

"Sorry about that. I didn't want to be late," Gail said. Kat nodded, but held up one finger as she listened to something on her headset.

"Please stay in here until I come back to get you," Kat said. "We want to capture that first moment when you and your match see each other."

Gail wanted to groan. But she knew deep down that if she stayed in her rut any longer, her life would be nothing but work, and her dreams of a family and all that went with it would never be realized.

She stared at herself in the mirror as she waited for the hair and makeup person to arrive. Her thick, curly hair with its wild, out-of-control style framed her face. She reached up and pulled her hair back…that was how she usually wore it for work. Because let's face it, she thought, her unruly hair didn't scream sexy and single.

A man and woman approached her. "Hello, Gail. I'm Mona, and this is Pete. We're going to be doing your hair and makeup. Just sit back and relax."

Gail did just that, wondering what she'd gotten herself into. She'd wanted a man to spend her holidays with instead of being home alone, which might have been fun for Kevin in the *Home Alone* movies, but for her, a grown woman, it had been…lonely. She craved the perfect Christmas, for example, and images of it played in her mind like home movies. She was in the business of image and reality, so why couldn't she create the perfect image and reality for herself?

She'd developed a PR plan to take herself from a business success to a personal success. She was very good at enacting her plans, so she had no doubt this one would work. Of course, she hadn't expected Willow to love the idea so much that she'd turn it into a reality TV show.

"Okay, we're done," Mona said.

They turned her back to face the mirrors. Her thick, unruly hair had been straightened and styled to brush her shoulders. Her eyes were bigger than she'd ever seen them before. Her lips were so large and perfect. She'd had no idea a little lipstick and eye shadow could make her look like this. She didn't recognize herself.

"What do you think?" Pete asked.

"I don't look like me," she said.

"Sure you do, honey. Just not the you that is usually in the mirror," Mona said.

And that had been exactly what she'd wanted. "What do I do now?"

"Wardrobe," Pete said. "Your dressing room is over there."

She walked over to the tiny dressing room in the corner. There was a woman sitting there reading a paperback book—one that Gail had just finished. This was the life she was used to, and Gail felt as though she could just sit here for a few minutes. The woman put the book down and smiled at her. "Looking good."

"Thanks."

Gail had the feeling that Alice must have experienced when she fell down the rabbit hole, because twenty minutes later she stood in front of a full-length mirror in a couture gown by Jil Sander. The well-fitting top came to a V, revealing her cleavage, while the peplum skirt gave her hips a flattering fullness, hitting her midthigh. She looked sexy and glamorous, two things she'd never felt before.

Kat came back and signaled that it was time to go. Gail realized her hands were sweating and started to wipe them on her skirt but stopped—this gown cost more than her entire wardrobe. She was going to mess this up. No matter how much magic these stylists had done to her outside, inside she was still the woman who'd spent all of her time working. She had no idea how to make real small talk. This was a mistake.

"Two minutes until you will go into the 'confessional,' then it's down to the ballroom, where you will meet your date, Ms. Little," Kat said.

Gail was nervous. And that wasn't like her. She wasn't the type of woman who let anything stand in her way once she'd made up her mind.

A tech guy in black pants and a polo shirt came over and attached a microphone to her collar. She should approach this the same way she approached a client at her PR firm who needed more exposure. She'd smile and pretend the glam woman staring back at her in the mirror was who she really was.

She stood up and walked over to the entrance to the small room that had been made out of moveable walls and pipe and drapes. No privacy at all. But then, that was reality television.

"Just push the button and start talking. Don't worry—if you mess up, just start over. We're going to edit it," Kat said.

"What am I supposed to say?"

"Tell us what you are thinking before you meet your match."

She stepped into the room and walked over to the camera. She sat down in front of it and pushed the record button. There was a small monitor where she could see herself, which just made her uncomfortable, so instead she stared into the lens of the camera.

"Let's see…. I'm Gail Little and I own a public relations firm. I am beyond nervous.

"That's it. I signed up with Matchmakers Inc., because I didn't want to let another year go by without meeting someone. I work all the time and don't meet many single men in my job," she said. Then she took a deep breath. She was rambling.

"I'm anxious to find out more about the man that has been picked for me." She pushed the stop button and got up and walked out of the room.

She'd done the best she could. She turned resolutely to walk back to the makeup area. "All done?" Kat asked.

"Yes."

"This way, then. Your date is waiting for you."

They stepped into the hallway and the soundman checked her microphone. "Bob is the cameraman who will be shooting you. He will be in front of you as we enter the ballroom. Don't look at Bob. Instead, look toward the table where your match is waiting."

"Okay," she said. Bob waved at her from the end of the hallway.

"Walk toward Bob and then enter the ballroom. It's been set up for an intimate dinner for two. As soon as we are out of the shot, I will signal you. Just start walking."

Kat and the soundman joined Bob at the end of the hall, and it felt like an eternity before she was given the signal to go. She walked down the hallway, feeling silly that they were taping her walking. But she forgot about that when she stepped into the ballroom.

There were a few production people in the room as well as a man who stood with his back toward her. But she was distracted when Jack Crown stepped in front of her.

"Hello, Gail," he said.

Jack Crown was gunning to beat out Ryan Seacrest for hosting the most shows on TV and was obviously the host of this one. He'd been an all-state athlete in high school and then went on to win the Heisman Trophy in college. He'd been a first-round draft pick and then suffered an agonizing injury in his very first professional football game. But he'd smiled up at the cameras and just shrugged his massive shoulders saying that America hadn't seen the last of him, and he'd been right. He started showing up on television regularly hosting reality shows for the Discovery Channel.

"Hello, Jack," she said. "What are you doing here?"

"I'm the host of the show. I'll be chatting with both of you at the end of your dates."

"Okay," she said. "Now?"

"No, we want to see how you both react to meeting each other," he said, stepping away. Her date had large, strong shoulders that tapered down to a lean waist, which she could see because he wore a well-fitted jacket.

"Stop," Willow, the producer, said, her voice loud in the quiet of the room. It was funny because Gail had never been at work with Willow before, and the booming voice didn't sound like her friend's. "You are going to see each other for the first time in just a moment. I want you both to look at each other and not the cameras. Kat, move her into position."

Kat directed Gail to a spot that was marked on the floor with tape. Gail stood so close to her match that she could smell the woodsy scent of his cologne. And she noticed his thick hair was a brown color with shots of golden-blond in it.

"We're ready to shoot now. Please turn and face your match," Willow said.

The man turned and Gail's breath caught. Then her heart sank. It was billionaire New Zealand hotelier and nightclub owner Russell Holloway. She recognized him from his constant exposure on TV and in magazines. He couldn't be her match. Surely this was a joke. He was a playboy with a reputation as a love-'em-and-leave-'em guy. Why would he go to a matchmaker?

Gail met the full force of Russell's gray gaze. His eyes were bright and intense, staring down at her. He didn't look as debauched as he should, she thought. He looked tanned, fit and healthy...too damned good for someone as bad as he was rumored to be.

"Gail Little," she said, holding out her hand. "I've heard a lot about you."

Dumb. Was that really the only thing her mind could come up with?

Russell laughed as he took her hand and kissed it. "Uh-oh, that doesn't sound promising. I know precious little about you, but I look forward to hearing your story from your own lips."

She licked her lips and stared up at him. Her eyes tracked down his face to the sharp blade of his nose and then the full, sensual mouth underneath. *Lips*...the word echoed in her mind, and all she could do was stare at his. She gave herself a mental shake. She wasn't going to be the latest to fall for this charming playboy. He was messing up her plans, and there was nothing fun about that.

Russell Holloway wasn't sure what type of woman he'd expected to be matched with, but he knew he hadn't anticipated Gail Little. She was beautiful, with her thick black hair brushing her shoulders and her big brown eyes that tempted him to get lost in them. Her figure was curvy and generous. If he were honest, she was exactly what he wanted physically. And she was classy. He couldn't remember the last time he'd met a woman like her.

"I'm Russell Holloway," he said, though he could tell she recognized him. She'd said that she'd heard of him.

"I know." Then she shook her head. "Despite how it may seem, I'm usually a bit wittier."

He chuckled. "First meetings can be a bit nerve-racking."

"Yes, they can."

She stared up at him and then flushed. "I don't know what to say."

"Then say nothing and let me enjoy the view. You're a very beautiful woman."

"I don't know about that. Should we take our seats at the table?"

"Not just yet," Russell said, linking her hand through his arm, leading her out of the ballroom and into the hallway.

He'd already arranged for the camera crew to follow them. Every detail had to go off smoothly. Russell had signed up with the matchmaking service to improve his reputation.

The Kiwi Klubs had had stagnate growth for the past

two years. They had started as destination clubs similar to Club Med. Attached to each of the hotels was an exclusive A-lister nightclub where people went to see and be seen. Russell was making a profit but he wanted to try something new, and the real money in destination vacations was in families. He wanted to open a family-friendly resort, but with his reputation that was easier said than done. He had a chance to buy a well-known family vacation company but the owner was balking at selling to someone like Russell—not from a business standpoint but from a reputation-based one. So he'd decided to try to change his image.

He'd already arranged with Willow and Conner Mac-Afee, Matchmakers Inc.'s owner, to give Gail a preview of the Gustav Klimt exhibit that would be opening here in the Big Apple Kiwi Klub on Wednesday. As a personal friend of Russell's, Conner had suggested participating in the show as a course of action to help Russell out.

"Where are we going?" she asked. "I think we are supposed to stay where we were."

"Afraid to get in trouble?" he asked.

"No. I just like to follow the rules," she said.

"I don't."

"Shocker," she said.

He laughed. She gave the impression of being very sure of herself and confident. Those were traits that he'd been hoping for in his match. "Don't fret, Gail, this side trip has been preapproved."

"Good," she said.

"Here we are," he said, opening a door that led into the mezzanine atrium. The hotel area was very modern and had large expanses of open wall space with a glass dome inspired by Van Gogh's *Stormy Night*. The floor was made of marble.

"This exhibit is opening on Wednesday, so we will be the first to experience it."

When he'd approved the design, he'd specified that the atrium be used to display art. He had wanted to capture the feeling of the Metropolitan Museum of Art and replicate it here. If he was going to get families and couples into his hotels, then he needed to give them something special.

"I love Klimt's work. I have a print of *The Kiss* hanging in my bedroom at home," she said.

Russell thought it interesting that Gail had chosen that piece to hang in her bedroom. In it, the man was completely wrapped around the woman, holding her face in his hands as he kissed her neck. Klimt's style was very sensual.

"Have you ever been kissed like that?" he asked.

She glanced up at him, a bit of shock in her eyes. "No. I don't think so. But I'm sure you have."

He arched one eyebrow at her. She didn't seem to like him very much. "A gentleman doesn't kiss and tell."

"But then, you never have been a gentleman," she said almost sharply.

"That's true," he acknowledged. "I'm not exactly the kind of man who's been circumspect in my relationships. But that's why I'm here."

"Truly?"

"Yes. I'm not on this show to play games with you, Gail. I'm looking for a match just like you are." He knew if he was going to be successful in changing his reputation, it had to start with Gail. If he couldn't convince her he wanted to change away from his bad boy image, the viewers at home wouldn't buy it either.

"I'm sorry if I jumped to conclusions," she said.

"You should be," he said, flirting with her.

The PA motioned for them to move, and Russell put his

hand at the small of Gail's back and steered her toward another framed picture. It was a portrait of a high-society woman. They stood in front of it for a long time.

"She reminds me of you," he said. It was a sensual portrait of a fully-dressed woman with an open bodice, just starting to reveal herself to the viewer.

"Did I mention that I don't fall for practiced lines," Gail said.

"What makes you think that was a line?" he asked.

"She's so sexy," Gail said.

"You are too," he said.

Gail gave him a *yeah, right* look, and Russell realized for the first time that he was dealing with Gail's future as well as his own. And though he'd decided to do this purely for business reasons, he was determined to give her the very best of himself—however little that might be.

He reached over to touch her face, but Gail drew back. Getting past his reputation was going to be harder than he'd expected. It had been too long since he'd moved in any circles other than those inhabited by his decadent friends.

"She's mysterious like you, as well. There is more to you than meets the eye," he said.

"And you're all flash, aren't you?" she asked.

"I'd like to hope not. Otherwise I'd be pretty boring."

"Well, no one has ever called you boring," she admitted.

Russell turned them both back toward the end of the hallway. He'd forgotten the cameras were there. He rarely let anyone distract him from his surroundings and was a bit surprised that Gail had.

"Okay, cut. Great job, you two. Jack, come on in," Willow said.

Jack joined them, and Russell was reminded that this was definitely a TV show. Jack shook his hand and Gail's.

"You two are doing great," he said.

"Thanks," Russell replied.

"Okay, we're ready to start shooting," Willow said from across the room.

"Now that you've finished your first date, what do you think of Matchmakers Inc.?" Jack asked.

"They saw what I wanted even though Gail isn't my normal date," Russell said. "I think that the matchmaker was very intuitive."

"And you, Gail?"

"Well, Russell is definitely the last guy in the world I would have expected, so in that respect they found me a man I couldn't find on my own."

Jack laughed and then Willow called, "Cut."

"Jack, we'll need you to finish shooting the intro. Russell and Gail, you are free to go back to the dining room, where a crew will tape you talking and eating." The crew started heading back in that direction.

"That should be exciting," Gail said, turning sharply and walking across the atrium.

"What's your hurry?" Russell asked.

"I want to talk to Willow before we film any more."

"Why?" Russell asked.

"I just need to confirm some details with her," Gail said.

"Are you going to try to back out of this?" he asked.

She shrugged. "Don't take it personally, but I'm not sure that you are at all the right person for me. I'm sure that this would be interesting viewing—the whole opposites attract thing—but I want more than interesting viewing."

She started to walk away, and Russell realized anew

how hard changing his reputation was going to be. "I'm not doing this for ratings."

She stopped and glanced back over her shoulder at him. "Why are you doing it?"

"We all have to grow up, and I'd say it's definitely my time."

He saw something change in her eyes and knew he had her. She wanted to see if he really was just the playboy, or if there was something more.

"Fine. I won't say anything to Willow until after this date. But I'm not going to make it easy on you. Finding a husband is my goal for this year, and I don't want to waste my time with someone who clearly isn't marrying material."

Clearly, this wasn't going to be as easy as Russell had hoped.

Two

Since the beginning, when Willow had decided to take Gail's personal life and make it into a reality television show, Gail had had a niggling doubt in the back of her mind that this wasn't going to work out. But she'd forked out a lot of money to the matchmakers, and she really wanted to find a man to share her life with.

Willow had thought the show would be intriguing because a lot of successful men and women were finding it harder to meet someone. Willow said that with the 24/7 workday, it was inevitable that no one would have time for courtship.

Gail agreed, which was why she'd gone to a matchmaker. But she'd never expected a man like Russell Holloway to need one. He could snap his fingers and have any girl he wanted at his door.

Russell wasn't the man for her. Of course, he was sexy as hell…but she wasn't looking for sexy. She was looking for the guy in the Ralph Lauren ad, she thought, the one with perfectly styled hair, wearing those polo shirts and standing in front of a mansion in the Hamptons. She wanted someone who could look the part and give her the fantasy of the perfect life that she'd always craved.

She wanted to relax and enjoy her time with Russell, but she was under the gun, so to speak. Her biological clock wasn't just ticking, it was winding down faster than most of her peers'. She had to see if Russell was going to be the right man for her. Could he be? Now she was beginning to wonder.

She was seated at a private table, waiting for him. He'd had to take a call before they started shooting. Gail had pulled out her iPhone, but really she'd told her assistant, J.J., to handle all emergencies tonight. She knew she'd never have a chance at making this a success if she was distracted with work.... Her mind began to wander.

Was there more to Russell than met the eye? She knew there had to be, but thanks to years in publicity, she knew that usually what was beneath a shiny surface was less than appealing.

Russell rejoined her, and there was a lot of movement around them as sound techs and makeup people made them both camera ready.

"If my mates saw me with this makeup on, they'd never let me live it down," he said.

She had to smile. "It's just part of the package for being on TV, part of the glam life all celebs have to endure."

"Never thought I'd be part of any 'glam life,'" he said.

"Why not? You seem very at home in the jet set." Just this morning, she'd seen a picture of him on a yacht with two Spanish royals on one of the gossip sites she monitored for her clients.

"It's not really my thing," he said. "I like to travel and

I ski and yacht and go to club openings, but a lot of that is for my business. To keep it in the public eye."

"Yet you get a lot of newspaper and internet coverage," she said. She didn't follow him, so she had no idea when the intense media scrutiny had started, but she'd be willing to bet it had been there since he'd become successful in the hotel world. He had looks that no woman would resist.

"I do, but I really don't court that," he said.

Their food was delivered, and Gail found herself unable to stop looking at Russell. She had met so many people who'd needed to have their images cleaned up that she freely admitted she often saw the worst in someone. But she wanted to give Russell a chance, not simply to be fair to him, but also for her own sake. She'd invested a hell of a lot more than money in these dates; she'd kind of thought of them as her last chance.

"You're staring at me," he said.

"You are a very pretty-looking man," she said, being glib because that was easy when she didn't want to be honest.

"Pretty…isn't that a word for girls?" he asked.

"No. Boys can be very pretty." And he was, with that classic jawline and thick brownish-blond hair. But he was also a bit on the rugged side, thanks to that square jaw and a small scar on the bottom of his face. His face had character, but she wasn't sure if it was good. He had the build of a boxer and carried himself like a man who'd lived life—a very upper-crust one, but still, there was more to him than money.

"Well," he said, lifting one eyebrow sardonically, "thanks, I guess."

She smiled at him. He was an easy man to talk to, and though she was giving him the fifth degree in the hope of catching him out in a lie, she liked him. "I keep looking for some indicator that you are being honest with me."

"And?" he asked.

"I'm simply not sure yet. But I think it's making me overanalyze your every action," she admitted. But if she was honest, she did that with everyone. She'd always spent a lot of time thinking about why people did things. It didn't bring her any closer to really understanding them, but she tried.

"Then I'm not doing my job," he said. He leaned in, and she could smell that one-of-a-kind, spicy aftershave of his. "Am I boring you?"

"No, you are not boring me at all. Tell me why you are here," she said. It was a question she'd originally planned on asking her date before she knew it was Russell. In fact, she now made the snap decision to treat him the way she would have treated John Doe if that's whom she'd been matched with. No need to change just because he was Russell Holloway, international billionaire and playboy.

He leaned back in his chair and looked into her eyes. "It's time to settle down. I set out to make my fortune and a name for myself. I think we can both agree that I've done that."

"I'm not buying that as the entire story. There must be more," she said.

He laughed and tipped his head to the side, studying her, and she felt a little exposed for a moment, as though he was trying to see past the makeup and the facade to the real woman underneath. "The truth is that I like the party lifestyle, but it has lost its charm. I want to have a partner I can share all my life with, not just a couple of days."

She wanted to believe him. Who wouldn't? It was every young girl's dream to have a playboy like him say he wanted to settle down, and to be the lucky one he chose. "I can understand that, but marriage?"

"Why do I seem so debauched to you?" he asked.

"You don't," she said, realizing she was being harder on him than she would have been on any other man. And she knew it was because she was mad. Mad that she'd been matched to this man and now had to make the best of the situation.

"I'm sorry. Tell me about your family," she said.

"I had a traditional upbringing, and though my parents are gone, I know they wanted me to get married and have kids someday."

He had a pensive look on his face, and he turned away from her for a moment. She felt bad about the way she'd been questioning him. He obviously had a reason for going to the matchmaking service just as she had, and she should respect that.

She cleared her throat, and he turned his attention back to her. "You have kids, right?"

"No," he said. "There have been paternity suits that I have settled out of court, but I have no kids."

"Why not just make a family of those blended children?" she asked. What did he mean by settling paternity suits but not having any kids? She wanted to know more but this first date wasn't the time to ask questions.

"It's not feasible, since they aren't mine," he said.

"What do—"

"Enough questions—it's my turn. Why did you go to a matchmaker?" he asked, turning that direct, silver gaze of his on her. Suddenly she wanted to go back to being anonymous. She wanted to be the one in control, and she wasn't the least bit interested in sharing that control with him.

She fidgeted a little in her chair. She didn't want to tell

him about herself. "The simple answer is that it's the next step for me. I have a successful business and a good life."

"Sounds idyllic, but since you are here with me, something must be missing," he said.

"Yes," she said.

"It makes sense," he said. "And I understand where you are coming from."

"Do you?" she asked. It was hard for her to believe that she had much in common with this man. Odd to her that the two of them were at the same point in their journeys. But they were here together and, no matter how wrong that felt to her, she decided she'd make the best of it for now.

"Yes, when I was young I knew what I wanted and went after my goals with single-minded intensity. I worked hard and played hard and then one day…"

"You woke up and realized that you had everything?" she asked.

"Yes. But I wasn't satisfied."

"Me either," she said. Maybe she didn't want to see the man behind the image. Because now that she saw him expressing the same doubts that she had, she was starting to like him.

Like was too tame a word. She was attracted to him and wanted to find something—anything—that would give her a reason to stay on this show with him. The legal reason—the contract she'd signed—wasn't enough. But hearing him express himself this way…it was appealing.

"You're staring at me again," he said. "I'm trying not to let it go to my head, but you're making me feel irresistible."

"You'll have to get used to it, if you keep surprising me."

"Then I will, because I intend to keep you off balance," he said.

"Why?"

"That's the only way I'm going to get to know the real Gail," he said.

"And that's important?" she asked. She wasn't too sure she wanted anyone to know the real woman she was.

"Infinitely," he said. "I think that is the only way that you are going to let me know you trust me. I mean, really trust me."

"I don't trust easily," she admitted. "I guess that's another reason I've gone to a matchmaker."

"You've been burned by a man before?" he asked, leaning closer.

"Yes," she said, putting her head down and remembering that past love. Joe hadn't meant to hurt her—she was still sure of it—but he'd been too much into what Joe wanted to never realize that he was stepping on her dreams to achieve his own.

Russell nodded and took her hand. "I know there isn't anything I can say right now that you'd believe, but I do want to be very sure you understand I'm not like any other man you've had in your life before."

"I already knew that," she said with a grin.

"It's my pretty face, right?" he asked with a sexy smile that sent shivers of awareness down her spine.

"Okay, that's a wrap on dinner. Let's get you two up to the rooftop," the director said. The crew all bustled around them, and Gail realized she'd had enough. This matchmaking thing was going to take some getting used to. Add to that the cameras, and it was her definition of a nightmare.

Jack came back over and spoke to them again about their impressions of the first date. Gail was unsure what to say. She mumbled something and then thankfully was motioned off camera so Jack could talk to Russell. She stood to the side watching Russell and hoping this wasn't a huge mistake.

Had she really thought she'd find Mr. Right like this? Through a matchmaking service that she'd found off an internet ad? But, really, what had her alternatives been? She'd dated all the guys she knew. Willow and Nichole had even tried fixing her up, but that had led to nothing permanent.

"Are we going to jump?" Gail asked.

"Not a bad idea. I guess that's how we will get some ratings for the show," Russell said. "I can see the headlines now. Respectable woman pushes rogue Kiwi playboy off roof in hopes of finding a better match."

Gail had to laugh. "I won't push you…yet."

"I guess I better step it up in the charm department," he said.

Before she could answer, Kat was back and taking her by the arm. "Chat on camera, guys. We need you on the roof now."

They were escorted to a private elevator and soon were on the rooftop helipad, where a chopper waited for them. "Is this for us?"

"Surprise," Russell said. "I thought an evening ride over Manhattan would be nice."

"I am surprised," Gail said. "I've always wanted to do this."

"Good. Also, cameras can't come with us, so we will have some time alone to get to know one another."

Gail didn't say anything else as their microphones were removed and they were escorted to the chopper. She saw the cameraman at a distance, no doubt filming them so they'd have something to show later, but she was relieved that they were going to be alone.

Russell gallantly helped her into the chopper and was

seated next to her a short time later. He handed her some headphones, which she donned, and then she adjusted her microphone. "I'm sure I look pretty glamorous with these on my head."

"You look great," he said.

In a matter of minutes, they were in the air and flying over Manhattan. Russell's voice was soft and intimate in her ears.

"When I first came to the States, I wanted to make my mark here. We started in Vegas because that suited the Kiwi Klubs' reputation, but I wanted to own a building in New York City," he said.

She looked over at him. "How did you get started?"

"With a small run-down hotel in Sydney," he said. "I won it in a high-stakes poker game."

"I though you were a New Zealander from the South Island?"

"I am. I left home when I was sixteen and never looked back," he said.

"I didn't see any of that on the internet when I was reading up on you," she said. "I'm embarrassed to say, I only know the gossip I've read about you."

He shrugged. "That's the easy stuff to know."

"But is it true?" she asked. "I've been in PR long enough to know that sometimes bad publicity can work in your favor."

"Exactly," he said. "I'm known for having rich and famous friends and for being a bit of a player, and that is exactly what my clientele wants."

"So why change now?" she asked. "Is this more than a publicity stunt?"

"Of course it is. I'm not going to get married as a stunt," he said.

"Many have done it before. Even if they weren't just

for show, marriages of convenience have been around for centuries."

"I'd find it very convenient to have to look at you at breakfast every day," he said in that flirty way of his.

"Me, too, but I need more sustenance than flash," she said.

"Don't we all. It's easy to think that something or someone flashy has what you need, but after a short while you find that's not true," he said.

She glanced over at him. Surprised to hear something so…well, *deep* from him.

He arched an eyebrow at her. "I'm not just a playboy."

She smiled at him. "You couldn't be and be on the cover of *Fortune* magazine."

"True. What about you?"

"Me?" she asked. "I'm not flashy at all. This is me at my most flashy."

He chuckled. "I'm not shocked. You strike me as someone who is very sure of herself and where she is going."

She shrugged one shoulder. "I love to have a plan and then execute it. But when I have to depend on someone else…well, let's just say sometimes things get messed up."

"Like this?"

She bit her lower lip. She didn't want to lie to him, but then she had nothing to lose. Russell wasn't the kind of guy she usually went for, so being brutally honest wasn't going to cost her anything. "Yes, like this situation with you. I mean, I planned to go to the matchmaker and find the perfect guy. I have a checklist in my head with all his qualities."

"And I don't measure up?" he asked. "That's not fair, Gail. You don't know if I have those qualities yet."

"You're right. But you are flashy," she said with a grin. "And I'm a bit afraid to risk getting to know the real man."

"I can understand that. I'm coming at this from the opposite point of view. If you aren't the woman I think you are…then I'm screwed."

She laughed at how he'd said that. "I guess we both are."

He reached over, took her hand in his and lifted it to his mouth, rubbing his lips over the back of her knuckles. "I don't want that. Let's start over. I'll try to be more the man of your dreams and you can…"

"Yes?"

"Give me a chance and not judge me so harshly."

"I will try. It's one of my worst faults," she said, liking the way her hand felt in his.

"What is?"

"Not being able to accept failure."

"In others?" he asked, rubbing his thumb over the back of her hand before slowly letting it go.

Chills spread up her arm, and she knew she wanted to keep touching him. It was unexpected. She didn't know why and couldn't really explain it, but there was something about Russell Holloway that made her forget about lists and plans.

"And in myself," she said softly, almost to herself. But she knew he'd heard her because he nodded.

"I'll try not to let you down," he said.

And just like that, she was hooked on giving him a chance. She wanted to guard her emotions, to warn her heart to be careful where he was concerned, because her common sense told her there was more to Russell's move than just his wanting to change. But she couldn't help herself. For these next six weeks she wanted to be the kind of girl who'd allow herself to be caught up in a man. Even if she knew he was at his core a bad boy who would probably break her heart.

* * *

Russell knew that he was luckier than many men. He had his secrets and more than his share of hardships, but life had been good to him. And this was one of the moments when he realized he'd gotten lucky. He needed a woman like Gail and here she was, dropped into his lap.

Her skin was soft and smooth and he liked touching her, holding her hand. But he didn't want to crowd her. She smelled nice and clean, a pretty floral fragrance that he knew he'd remember long after he left her tonight.

"Thank you, Russell," she said.

"For?"

"This ride. It's really nice being up here, and I needed some time away from the cameras."

"I did too. I'm not used to conducting my dates in front of an audience," he said. Even though most of the women he dated were famous and they always had their pictures in the tabloids, Russell did try to avoid the spotlight.

"Me either. In fact, this is the first date I've been on that has felt this…high profile," she said. "Not at all what I expected."

"Is it on your list?" he asked.

"What list?"

"The Mr. Right checklist," he said. He liked the forthright way she spoke and how she always looked him straight in the eye when she talked to him. It made him aware that she was weighing everything he did and said. He needed to be careful to watch himself around her.

"Well…it's not real. Just a bunch of feelings and qualities that I think a man should have that would be compatible with mine."

He tipped his head to the side. "That's a checklist."

She shrugged delicately, drawing his gaze to her shoulders. They were left bare by the sleeveless dress she wore.

Her arms were toned and muscled, so she must work out, he guessed.

"You're right. It is a list. I'm looking for someone with a good job."

"Easy! Check one off for me."

She smiled at him. "I'll give you that."

"What else?"

"He has to be…committed to the person he's dating."

"Ah. That one will be harder to convince you of, won't it?"

"Yes. You aren't exactly known for monogamy."

"I am here, aren't I?"

"Yes. So that one is a maybe," she said.

"What else?"

"Um…" She hesitated, then a pretty pink blush spread up from her neck to her cheeks.

"What could be next?" he asked. "Why are you so shy now?"

She wrapped her arms around her waist and looked out at the skyline of Manhattan. He saw the reflection of her face in the window of the chopper as she absently brought her hand up to toy with the charm on the gold necklace she wore.

"I have to be attracted to you. A healthy sex life is on my checklist."

"When the time is right, Gail, you will have no doubts that I can fulfill your needs on that count."

She turned back around to face him. Her thick black hair with the headphones on it made her seem smaller somehow. In the intimacy of the chopper, she didn't seem as tough as she had in the ballroom when first seen her. Her mouth was full, and he couldn't help but keep his eyes on her lips. He wanted to taste them. He needed to kiss her just to prove to himself that, even though she felt different to him, she wasn't. He desired her. He knew that, but he wanted it to be just the normal lust he'd feel for any attractive woman.

Somehow though, in these close quarters with just the soft sound of her voice in his ears and her leg brushing his, it felt different. He felt different. He wanted to imagine he could check off all the qualities on her Mr. Right checklist, and he didn't know why that mattered.

He leaned in close and she just stared at him. The microphone was in front of her face, and he reached to push it up and out of his way. He did the same with his mic, and then touched her face. Her skin was smooth and cool to the touch.

He let his thumb move lower to touch her lips. He traced them: the small indentation at the top and the full, fleshy lower one. Then he closed the small distance between them and kissed her. Just a simple brushing of their mouths at first, and then he slipped his tongue in over her teeth until he tasted her.

He tipped his head to the side; he wanted more of her. The thought that she was just like any other woman disappeared in an instant. This was more than lust. He lifted his hands, tangling them in her thick hair as he tried to get more out of the kiss. Gail's hands fell to his shoulders, softly at first, and then as she moved closer to him, her grip got tighter.

He pulled back and took a deep breath. She said something, but he couldn't hear it because her microphone wasn't in position. He brought it down and she shook her head. "I didn't expect that."

"I didn't either."

She wrinkled her brow. "You were the one who kissed me."

"I was trying to prove something to myself."

"What?"

"That you were like every other woman I've ever kissed," he said.

She narrowed her gaze. "That's—

"Don't get your back up. You weren't. I don't know why," he said, genuinely perplexed. One of his good friends had married last year and Russell, while happy for him, hadn't understood how one woman could be that important. Now he had an inkling of what Cam Stern had been experiencing and Russell didn't like it for himself.

"Is that supposed to be a compliment?" she asked.

"Hell. No, it wasn't. I don't know what it was supposed to be. I only know that I have no idea how to proceed with this."

"Why not?" she asked.

He shook his head. He wasn't supposed to be this attracted to his match. But his blood was pounding in his veins and he had to shift his legs to make room for his growing erection. He wanted her. He wanted her right now. But that wasn't going to happen tonight. He needed to ensure that this matchmaking thing worked first, and sleeping with her tonight would pretty much send her running for the hills.

Three

Gail didn't know what had happened, but somehow in the last thirty minutes, Russell Holloway had started to become real to her. He was no longer that bad-boy cad whom she could keep her distance from. Instead she'd kissed him.

Oh, yes, she had. That was the most daring thing she'd done since skinny-dipping in high school. She shook her head; she had become a very staid person. In fact, it had been almost seven months since her last kiss.

Now her lips still tingled from the contact with Russell's. And she wanted more than just a few kisses. She wanted to feel his strong chest against her breasts and his arms wrapped around her.

She had a feeling that Russell knew how to use his body for maximum effect, and she was definitely ready for more. But that wasn't smart. She prided herself on making the "right" choices, but now she wanted to just forget that and do what *felt* right.

So what?

She'd been smart her entire life, and look where it had gotten her. She was alone and doing silly things like signing up for matchmaking services and reality-TV shows. She wanted something—someone—different, and Russell certainly was that.

"You're staring at me again," he said with that little half smile of his that she was getting very used to seeing. He used it as a shield to seem open and friendly, but she knew it was a mask.

"That is entirely your fault," she said. "If you'd just act like I expected you to, then I could walk away and pretend I gave this a chance."

"Where would you walk to?" he asked. "If you are on this show, I'm guessing you are out of options."

"Very true," she said. "I guess I'd go back to my safe little world where everything fits neatly in its place."

"So I no longer fit in my place?" he asked her.

Frankly, she wasn't too sure what she'd do with Russell in his place. She wasn't cut out to date a jet-setting playboy, and no matter what the matchmaker thought, Gail knew he wasn't right for her.

"No, you don't," she said.

"What am I doing wrong?" he asked.

She nibbled on her lower lip and tasted him. "Kissing me."

"You didn't like it?" he asked. "I can try to improve my technique."

"I liked it too much," she said. "Don't be offended—"

He leaned down and arched one eyebrow at her in a way that made her feel as though she was amusing him. "Saying that pretty much guarantees I will be."

She smiled at him. "I guess so, but I expected your kiss to be practiced and kind of mechanical…."

"Glad to disappoint," he said.

She wrinkled her nose at him and mock-punched him. "I'm not letting my guard down, no matter how charming you act. I'm not sure about you."

"I wouldn't expect you to let your guard down. But there is one thing you should know."

"And that is…?" she asked.

"I don't lose," he said with a full-on, smug grin.

She wasn't too sure she wanted him to look at this as some kind of competition, and it was telling that he had done so. "I don't want you to lose. In fact, I want us both to get what we want."

He leaned back against the seat and crossed his arms over his chest, glancing out the window as the chopper pilot made his way back to the helipad on top of the Big Apple Kiwi. "That came out wrong, didn't it?"

"Only if you think of me as a prize," she said. "We're both feeling our way here. I'm not judging you."

He shook his head and leveled that steady gray gaze of his on her. "I think you are. You'd have to be. Otherwise, how will you be sure I'm not the player you've read about."

That insight was enough for her to continue to relax her guard. He knew that he wasn't just starting a new relationship and maneuvering through the normal obstacles that most couples experience. They had the added pressure of his being so unlike her Mr. Right.

She knew that she'd designed her list based on a fictional guy. Her father had divorced her mother when Gail was eight, so she only had vague impressions of him at home. Her mother had dated but never remarried, so Gail was pretty much left with movies and books to form her opinions of what she wanted in a man. Well, that and the men she'd dated, who'd left her wanting more.

"I'm aiming for a win-win here," she said at last, because, if she was honest, she had no idea what else to say.

"Me too," he said. "Once we land, do we have to do more camera work?"

"I'm not sure. I think they will tell us when we come down. Why?" she asked.

"If not, will you join me for a nightcap?"

She would have said no just twenty minutes ago, but now she wanted to spend more time with him to talk to him, and get to know his point of view. See how he really viewed the world. His public image was different from this private man, and she was determined to find out how much so.

She took a deep breath. It was easy to say she wanted to change and was willing to put herself out there, but the reality was so different. In her fantasy date, the man was everything that Hollywood and romance novels had groomed her to expect. But Russell was a mixture of those fantasies and reality.

She had to decide if she was ready to step out of those expectations and into Russell's world. She was. She wouldn't have signed up with a matchmaker otherwise. "Yes."

"Good. I knew that this was going to be a good thing," he said.

"Matchmaking?" she asked. "It's strange. I'm really not sure if it's going to work out or not. When I saw the ad for the service, it was New Year's Eve and I'd had a little too much champagne."

"And a bad date?"

She shook her head. "Nope. I was all alone and I resolved that I wouldn't be next New Year's Eve."

"Well you've gone a good route to find a mate. Match-making is an old tradition," he said.

"Even in Australia?" she asked. She wasn't that well traveled and didn't know what the customs were in other countries.

"I'm from New Zealand," he said. "But, yes, even there. Some of the women in my town were mail-order brides."

"Did you have any doubts about doing this?" she asked. She had been unsure as soon as she'd signed up. Writing the check had been easy, but as soon as she'd walked out the door of Matchmakers Inc., she'd started to feel so vulnerable and scared. At least the fee had been refunded once she'd been selected for the TV show.

"Lots of them, but then I thought, if a woman was brave enough to do this, I could handle it. Having another person pick a date for you isn't any worse than meeting someone in a bar," Russell said.

"I've never met a guy in a bar. Most of the men I dated were from work or classes."

"Somehow that doesn't surprise me," he said. "You don't seem like the type of woman who'd allow a man to pick her up in a bar."

"Why don't I?" she asked.

"You wouldn't have time to ask all your questions. Most men are looking for a quick score," he said.

He looked over at her, and she wondered if she'd revealed something she shouldn't have. She knew she didn't always say the right thing with men. But then she took a deep breath as the chopper banked for its landing, and she saw her own reflection in the window. She was on a matchmaking reality television show with a billionaire playboy.... There was nothing familiar about this scenario, and she was going to just let it play out.

"What are you thinking?" he said, his voice intimately deep in her ears, thanks to the headphones.

"Just how unreal this entire thing is," she said. "Not reality at all."

He laughed. "I agree. But I don't mind it. Dating hasn't worked out for either of us in the real world, so this might actually work."

She wasn't betting on it. They landed and took off their headphones, as the pilot turned off the helicopter.

"Do we have to tell them we kissed?"

Russell caressed her arm and linked their fingers together. "That can be our secret."

With those words, he made them a couple. They had a secret that was just between them and, in a night of showy emotion and put-on romance, it was the first genuine thing to happen.

"Okay," she said. "I like the idea of that."

"Good. I like the idea of you and me," he said.

She did too. But why? She wanted to figure out what it was about Russell that drew her in so deeply, but she had a feeling that the emotions he brought to the fore in her weren't going to be logical.

"Ready to face the cameras again?"

"Yes," she said. And she was definitely ready to get to know this man better, once filming stopped for the night and they were on their own.

She really liked Russell when they were alone.

Russell listened to the producer talking to Gail, and every once in a while, he heard her laugh. The sound was full of joy, and he could tell that she was enjoying whatever they were talking about. She was relaxed with Willow and her guard was down. Russell realized he still had a long way to go to get to know the real Gail Little.

"How's matchmaking going for you so far?" Conner MacAfee asked as he came up beside him.

"Not bad," he said.

"Good," Conner said. "You know Matchmakers Inc. has a one hundred percent success rate, right?"

"Do you?"

"Yes, we do."

"Did you do anything differently for us because of the TV show?"

Conner shook his head. "No way. We can't compromise our policies, even for a show. I'm hoping to get some business out of this, and I can't if we don't do what we normally do for our clients."

"Point taken. Do you know anything about Gail?" he asked Conner. He figured it was a fair enough question, given that she had heard of him.

"No. I really don't get involved in the matching. I just run the company," he said. He straightened his tie and glanced around the room. "I have to use my MBA from Harvard somehow."

"Don't brag," Russell said with a grin.

"What's the use in having one if you can't tell people about it?" Conner said.

"Why do you own a matchmaking company?" Russell asked. His friend was one of the smartest business minds he'd ever encountered. Russell had always thought it was an odd thing for Conner.

"It was my grandmother's business and I inherited it. I figured it wouldn't make money and I could take it as a tax loss, but in fact the opposite was the case," Conner said.

"The market can be unexpected. I'm trying to diversify now to make sure we have more of a toehold in other segments," Russell said. That had been one of the reasons why he'd agreed to be on the show. He needed potential investors to see that he was a changed man.

"No kidding. We added an exclusive wife-finder for some of our more eccentric customers," Conner said.

"What does that mean?" Russell asked.

"We vet the woman and send her to the client, and he approves her and marries her without any dating. It's a very new service and a niche market. But a very profitable one."

"That's interesting," Russell said. He guessed that everyone was scrambling in this new economy to figure out ways to stay ahead.

"Do you need anything from me?" Conner asked.

"No. I'm good. Poker on Thursday night?"

"Definitely. I want a chance to win back some of my money."

"Good luck with that. The cards favor me and always have."

"I know. I remember when we first met and you'd win enough money at the tables in Monaco to make your payroll."

"Those days are long behind me," Russell said. "But my ability at the poker table hasn't diminished."

"It might have. I feel the need to remind you whose country you are in," Conner said.

"I haven't lost yet," Russell said.

"That only means you are due for a fall," Conner said as he walked away. Russell watched his friend leave and took a deep breath. The air was chilly this evening but not cold. He suddenly felt a sense of peace he hadn't felt in a long time.

The production crew left the rooftop as a group. He and Conner made their way toward the elevators, with Gail and Willow following them. They were still talking.

"I got a call from a friend of yours," Conner said, turning to the women.

"Mine?" Willow asked.

"Yes, Nichole…I can't remember her last name. She wants to interview me about Matchmaker Inc."

"She works for *America Today* so she's legit," Willow said.

The elevator arrived.

"Do you want to chat about it quickly?" Willow asked.

"I'd like that," Conner said. "See ya later, Russell."

Russell waved goodbye to his friend as the doors opened. Dylan, his executive assistant, was on the elevator, a concerned look on his face.

"Hiya, boss. We have a situation," Dylan said, stepping out of the elevator.

"I'll leave you to it," Gail said, backing away from the two men.

"Wait, Gail. Are we still on for that nightcap?" he asked.

"Yes. The lobby bar?"

"Sounds good. Twenty minutes?"

"Yes," she said, getting on the elevator.

Russell waited until the doors closed before asking Dylan, "What is so important it needs my attention?"

"Penny Thomson is in the lobby demanding to see you. I tried to get her to wait in my office, but she wouldn't."

Great. Not what he needed this night, but he'd handle it. "Please make sure that Gail is taken care of until I'm done with Penny."

"I'm happy to, boss," Dylan said.

"Never mind, I'll talk to her. You tell Penny I'm on my way, but I will only meet with her in the office, not in the lobby," Russell said.

He took the elevator to the lobby and, once there, noticed that Willow had rejoined Gail and the two were talking.

"I'll try."

Dylan walked away, and Russell made his way to Gail. "I'm sorry, but I think my situation might take a little longer than anticipated. Can we meet in forty-five minutes instead?"

She flushed and looked at Willow. "We're having a drink. Is that okay?"

"Yes, that's fine. We want to capture the phases of your relationship, not every second. Enjoy yourselves."

Gail turned back to him with a slight smile on her face. "I'll be down there in forty-five minutes, then."

"Good."

Russell left the women and headed down to the lobby and the office behind the check-in desk. Dylan was standing outside of it when Russell approached.

"I always thought Penny would be nicer in person," Dylan said. "Sorry about that, sir. I should have kept that to myself."

"You probably should have, but I happen to agree that she can be a bit of a bitch."

Dylan nodded and then walked away.

Russell opened the door and saw Penny sitting on the edge of the desk. She had her iPhone in one hand and was delicately tapping out a message with the tip of one French-manicured fingernail.

"It's about time you got here. I've been tweeting about the inconvenience of waiting on a former lover."

"Nice. Good to see you too, Penny."

"Yeah, right. You made it clear you didn't want to see me again," she said.

She was a Hollywood starlet so beautiful that she'd floored Russell the first time he saw her. It had been impossible to think of anything but sex. But, after spending two days in bed with her, Russell knew it had been a mistake. Penny was vapid and so self-absorbed, it was impossible for her to be aware of anyone else.

"Stop tweeting. You always get yourself in trouble with that."

"Well, this time, Russell, you're the one who's going to be in trouble."

"Why, exactly? I thought we ended things amiably."

"Sure we did. But it turns out we have a few unresolved issues."

Russell realized as she talked that he couldn't wait to get away from her and back to Gail. He liked Gail's freshness and the way natural sensuality imbued her every movement, as opposed to Penny's in-your-face sexuality.

"Like what?"

"I'm pregnant," she said.

Russell shook his head. He'd settled a paternity suit when he was twenty-four and, ever since then, every time a past lover became pregnant he'd had to deal with this. "I'm not the father."

"I'm not so sure about that, Russell, and I'm going to be tweeting about it unless you do what you should," Penny said.

Penny's timing couldn't be worse. This was exactly what he didn't want to deal with today. He wanted to get back to Gail and continue courting her and wooing her. But instead… "I'm going to need to see proof you're pregnant, and then we need to do a paternity test."

"I don't know why. The baby is yours, and if you don't cooperate, I'm going to make life very difficult for you," she said.

He knew she meant it. He had to handle this delicately, because Gail was his chance at the future he wanted to have, and Penny was part of a past he was trying very hard to distance himself from.

Gail waited in the lobby bar for Russell, feeling just a little self-conscious that she was by herself. Honestly, she'd thought she'd mastered sitting alone in public a long time ago, but the truth was she hadn't. She didn't like it.

She felt someone watching her and glanced up to see Russell leaving the back office with his hand on the shoulder of a woman who looked familiar. Gail leaned forward and recognized her as Penny Thomson, rising Hollywood star and Russell's ex. Gail watched them for a minute before deciding that he wasn't the kind of guy she wanted to get to know better.

She knew any guy she dated would have an ex, but with another man, she wouldn't be competing against someone like Penny. This was a mistake, she thought. Her gut had said so from the moment she'd recognized Russell, but the romantic in her had been wooed during that chopper ride over Manhattan. Just because he had money and knew how to make the right reservations, it didn't mean he was capable of being the man she needed in her life. And Gail was on a tight timetable. She had these few months to find a man if she wanted to execute her "family" plan, including husband and, eventually, children.

Gail lifted the glass of soda water that she'd ordered and took a sip, trying to be disinterested. But she couldn't be. Russell and Penny looked perfect together. That would make great TV, she thought. The pretty blonde starlet and the ruggedly handsome man. Not at all like her and Russell.

She'd had enough of this. She was going home and she'd figure out a new plan in the morning. For tonight, she needed to get away from the Kiwi Big Apple and the man who'd almost made her…what? For a little while, she'd forgotten that she was really just a plain Jane. For a little while, she'd forgotten her common sense. Forgotten what was painfully obvious right now—that there was no way Russell would be interested in her, because he was used to a class of women that was out of her league.

She wasn't putting herself down, but was being realistic. She was never going to dress that overtly sexually or spend as much time on hair and makeup as Penny did. She was a normal woman with a job and a life. Not a sexual plaything whose sole purpose was to be seen on Russell's arm.

"I thought you were meeting Russell," Willow said, coming up to her table.

"I was," Gail said, tearing her eyes away from him to look at her friend. "He's over there."

Willow glanced at the couple and then back at Gail before sitting down. Willow had thick black hair that fell almost to her waist when she left it free, but normally she pulled it back in a ponytail. She was tall—almost five-eight—and had striking features. Staring at her friend, Gail almost thought Willow would look better on Russell's arm than she herself would.

"What's that about?" Gail asked, gesturing to the couple.

"I don't know. I think…he's not right for me. I can't keep doing this for five more dates. I know that it will screw up your show, but I just can't."

Willow nodded. "I get that. I will talk with Conner and ask that they get another match for you."

Gail shook her head. "No, I don't think that will work. I don't like having something so important out of my control."

"Then why did you sign up for it?" Willow asked. "You

were the one to start this—I mean everything, including the show. What's different?"

Gail took a deep breath. "I think I could really get hurt. I never considered that part in my plan."

"What part?"

"Emotions, Will. I could easily fall for Russell, with all his charm and bad-boy ways, but I don't know what he's doing on this show. He could be using me…. He probably is, and I have no way of shutting off my emotions."

Willow reached over and gave her a one-armed hug. "I'm not going to lie to you. I want you to keep dating him, because he's different than your usual guy and I think you need that. But I don't want to see you get hurt either."

Gail thought about that image in her head of the man she'd wanted to find, and realized that now she saw Russell. She liked him. He was funny and self-deprecating and oh so good at making her believe he wanted to change. But she'd just seen the proof with her own eyes. Even if he wanted to change, he wasn't going to be able to. He had past lovers who would always be a part his life. And Gail didn't know if she could deal with it.

"I'm jealous," Gail admitted to Willow.

"Of…?"

"Penny," Gail said. "Did you see them together? They belong with each other. I'm not as pretty as she is—"

"You're prettier," Willow said.

"And you're one of my best friends. You're biased."

"True, but I'm not going to lie to you. Yes, she is pretty in a very polished sort of way, but you have never been able to see how lovely you are. And I think that Russell will see that. He already has. He didn't have to invite you for a nightcap, did he?"

"No," Gail said, thinking about that kiss on the chopper. There was an attraction between them. Was she just a novelty to him? Someone different? She didn't know, and she didn't want to wait too long to find out.

"I...I think I'm going to have to back out of it," Gail said. "I can't take a chance that Russell is playing a game and using me as a pawn."

"Fair enough," Willow said. "I'll talk to Matchmakers Inc. and we'll find another couple to take over your slot."

"No," Russell said, surprising Gail and Willow as he walked up to their table.

"No?" Gail asked. "I don't think you get to decide for me."

"She has a point," Willow said. "We only want you on the show if you both are interested in going forward."

Russell pulled a chair up and sat down with them. "That makes perfect sense, but I'm not about to let Gail back out of this without at least talking to me," he said, turning to Willow. "Will you give us until the morning to let you know?"

"Yes," Willow said. "But I don't think Gail is going to change her mind."

"If I can't convince her to give me a chance, then it will be better to end it now," Russell said. "Let's get out of here."

Four

Russell needed Gail more than ever. The meeting with Penny had convinced him that, if he had any chance of changing his reputation and by default the reputation of the Kiwi Klubs, he needed someone like Gail. But his conscience wouldn't allow him to simply use Gail. He was going to have to be honest with her. And frankly, that scared him. He was used to behaving a certain way so that the public and the people around him believed him to be a playboy.

"I'm not sure that you can convince me to change my mind," Gail said, as they entered his penthouse apartment on the top floor of the Big Apple Kiwi.

One wall was floor-to-ceiling glass making the sweeping expanse of the city a backdrop for the apartment. She'd seen pictures of places like this in *Home & Garden* magazine, but frankly it felt staged. She didn't feel comfortable in the apartment or with Russell.

"If I can't, I don't deserve you," he said. "What can I get you to drink?"

"I'm getting tired, so I should skip the alcohol," she said. "It will put me to sleep."

"Fair enough. The living room is over there," he said, gesturing to the leather couches grouped together in a casual seating area. "Have a seat while I get myself a scotch."

She did as he directed, and Russell went to the wet bar to pour himself two fingers, neat. Gail looked lovely and a little lonely as she sat on one of the big, stuffed leather couches. His apartment was clearly a man's domain, and seeing her here made him realize the changes he would need to make to welcome a woman like her into his life.

He took a deep swallow of his drink and then set the glass down before going to join her. Convincing her he wanted to change was easy; he knew he'd done that already and had actually made her see beyond the tabloid reputation. Convincing her that he was really going to change would be harder. Hell, he wasn't even sure of it himself.

"This is a nice place," she said as he sat down.

"Thanks," he said.

"Has it been featured in any decorating magazines?" she asked, glancing around.

"Two. My decorator tries to use it to drum up business," Russell said.

"And has that worked?"

"So far it has. She's going to decorate my new home in the Hamptons for a twenty percent discount. I bet this place isn't as welcoming as your home," he said.

"But it suits your needs," she said. "You look very at home here."

"I am," he said. "Gail, I don't want you to back out of

the matchmaking now. I really need a woman like you in my life."

She shook her head. "You might want to think that, but I saw you tonight with Penny, and she fits you and your lifestyle."

"You have no idea how wrong you are. Penny is fun," he said. He refused to say anything bad about Penny, but wanted Gail to realize that Penny was used to playing a part…just as he was. "We are too similar. I need a woman like you, who forces me to be honest."

"Sounds like you need a mother," she said.

"That's not true. Most people—women—give me a pass. They accept my charm and my flirting with every woman as just the way I am. I have a feeling you wouldn't," Russell said, lifting one eyebrow at her in question.

"You've got that right. I'm not interested in a man who can't commit."

Russell knew that. He needed that. He needed Gail. He liked her, he wanted her and she'd be perfect for his image. Gail just had a totally respectable look. She was hardly the type of woman to be caught sunbathing topless on his yacht. Yet he sensed a passion in her, so it wasn't that she was a prude. Just that she was circumspect—something that had been lacking in his personal relationships up to this point. "Good. I'm too used to getting my way."

"Hence this conversation," she said. "Russell, I'm sure you're sincere in wanting to change, and maybe even in wanting to find a woman to spend the rest of your life with."

"But…?" he asked. He felt he should interject something to convince her to stick with the matchmaking, but he actually had no idea what argument would convince Gail to stay. She was still too much like a stranger to him.

"I'm not sure I'm the right woman for you. I don't know that I can help you make that change. But I do know that I like you. I can see myself easily falling for your lines, and if it turns out you're lying…"

"You're convicting me of something before I've even done it," he said.

"Based totally on your track record," Gail said. "Look at Penny tonight. What was she doing here?"

"She…she has a problem and she thinks I can help her," Russell said. How was he going to tell Gail that Penny thought she was pregnant and he was the father? That would be enough to send Gail running for the hills, but if he explained how he knew he couldn't be the father… It was too much for this early in the relationship.

"Tell me about it," Gail said.

"I'm not sure what is really going on. With Penny there's always a lot of drama and bold statements," Russell said.

"I can understand that," Gail said. She leaned back against the cushions. "I'm used to dealing with clients that are like that. But this isn't a business deal for me— this is my life and my future."

"I figured you have some experience of these sorts of things, being in PR. Right now, Penny's very excitable, but I think once she has some time to think, everything will be sorted out. I get that this is personal. It is for me too. I'm not playing a game with you."

"Are you sure?" she asked. "I want to believe you."

"Then believe me," he said.

"Do you need my professional help?" Gail asked. "I would take you on as a client even if the dating thing doesn't work out.… I'll even give you a twenty percent discount."

"Ha-ha. You are too generous," he said. "But I don't

need your professional help right now. I want your personal help, Gail. I want you to give me a chance to be the man of your dreams."

He felt a little hokey saying those words, but with Gail he knew they were important, and even though he was in uncharted territory, he was willing to go with his gut. It was his gut that had brought him his greatest business success, and he trusted it now to help him with Gail.

"Ugh!" She stood up, walked over to the windows and put one hand against the glass as she looked out. In the reflection, he saw the perplexed look on her face.

"What?" he asked, striding over to her.

She turned to face him, crossing both arms over her waist. "I know that I should say no and walk away now before we get too connected, but I can't."

"Why can't you?" he asked. He knew it was because he was saying the right things. He had always had good instincts about what a woman needed to hear in the beginning of a relationship. It was as they continued moving forward that he would run into trouble.

"Because you are total temptation for me, Russell," she said. "Don't let that go to your head. I just can't seem to resist the thought of really getting to know you."

"Good," he said. He knew that as they spent more time alone, he would be able to win her over. He'd always been good at knowing what to say to other people; it was how he'd convinced his backers to initially invest in his business. But with Gail, he knew he was going to have to do more than just say the right things. He was going to have to actually do the right things, and that was going to be hard.

He sat there staring at Gail and knew he was going to do whatever it took to get her to believe him, because without Gail, he'd have nothing but the empty existence he'd been living. And he didn't want to be stuck there any longer.

Gail didn't know if she was going to be up to the challenge of Russell, but then no man in the past had even made her want to try, and he did. She wanted to pretend it was just lust and attraction, because then she could say it was hormones and walk away. But there was more to her attraction to Russell than that.

"I will continue on the show and with our matchmaking dates, but only if you are completely honest with me, Russell. If I catch you out, I'm not going to give you any more chances."

She didn't trust easily to begin with, and a man like Russell—well, he just made her even more wary of believing him. He was used to playing fast and loose, and she wasn't. She felt off balance, and while part of her was excited by it, another part was warning her to run away.

"And I assume I can expect honesty from you at all times," he said.

"Yes, you can. I'm used to being on my own and keeping who I am very private, but I'll try to be open with you," she said.

Russell smiled at her, and she felt a little thrill run through her body. "I'll help you."

"Okay. So, that's settled. I think it's time for me to go home." She wanted to be back in her sanctuary with her comfy chairs and her quiet music. She wanted the scents of her home to soothe her, as they did every day when she returned.

"I don't want to let you go," he said.

"Well, I have to. I'm tired and I have an early appointment with a client. But I enjoyed tonight. It was different," she said.

"Indeed. I enjoyed your company, Gail," he said.

She liked the way her name sounded on his lips. His accent was part of it, but there was also the implicit intimacy in the way he talked to her. She felt special and singled out, and she liked that just a little too much.

"Thanks," she said. "Um…I guess I'll see you at our next date."

"I think so. I don't want to wait a week. If I call you, maybe we can find some time together," Russell said.

Gail nodded, but she knew that she needed some distance to figure out how to get to know Russell better without letting him too close to her.

"Call me," she said. She began walking to his door, but he was there first. He put his arm around her and held the door closed.

"Am I so scary that you have to run away?" he asked.

She turned under his arm so that she was facing him. He was so close she could see some stubble on his jaw. He smelled of expensive cologne and a natural male musk that was intoxicating. She thought how easy it would be to just give in to him in this moment. But she knew that she'd have to wake up in the morning, and she'd have regrets. She hated that feeling in her gut when she'd made a bad decision.

But there was no reason she couldn't at least touch him, now that they were away from the cameras and alone. She reached up and rubbed her finger over the light stubble on his jaw, liking the abrasion against her skin. She put her other hand on his chest and slowly slid it around to his back. He stood there, leaning over her, one hand against the door, the other hanging loosely by his side, and let her have her way.

"I'm not scared of you, Russell," she said, hoping that by saying the words out loud they would become the truth. But she knew that she was truly afraid of herself. Afraid of her own fantasies of Mr. Right, which had been in her heart and mind for so long that she was a little too eager to meet the man who would fulfill them. And there were parts of Russell that easily checked those boxes for her.

He leaned in closer. The spicy scent of his aftershave surrounded her, as did his body heat. She felt the exhalation of his breath against the hair at her temple, and she closed her eyes for a second. Pretended she didn't know his reputation and that he was just a man—a very good-looking man she wanted. Pretended there was no ticking clock for her to find Mr. Right. Pretended she could kiss him and then walk away.

She closed the gap between them and rubbed her lips over his. A light, gentle kiss was her intent, but Russell parted his lips, and she couldn't resist sneaking her tongue inside for just one taste. That was what she told herself. She'd kiss him quickly and turn away.

But his taste was addicting and one small kiss wasn't enough. She pulled herself closer to him and felt his hand come around her back. His hand was at her waist, squeezing her carefully as she rose on tiptoe and pressed her breasts against his chest.

He felt so good…too good. She didn't want to back away. She wanted to stay in his arms tonight and every night. And every night was the problem. She pulled back and moved away from him. Her lips were tingling, her skin was sensitive and her pulse was racing.

"Good night," she said, determined to leave now, before she did something completely stupid, like jumping in his arms and begging him to make love to her.

"I guess you really want to go," he said. "Is there nothing I can do to convince you to stay?"

She shook her head. There were things he could do, but she'd regret it in the morning, and she knew better than to give in to that type of temptation. Russell was dangerous to her because he could make her forget the reason she'd signed up with a matchmaker in the first place.

"You'd have to be a different man," she said at last.

He nodded and tightened his mouth as he stared down at her. He tucked a strand of hair behind her ear and leaned down so their eyes were level. "I will show you I can be."

He put his hand on the small of her back and walked her to the elevator. He rode down with her, and when they got to the lobby, he asked the concierge to call for his private car.

"I can take a cab," she said.

"Never. I take care of my women," he said.

"I don't want to be one of your women," she said. And that was the problem with Russell as far as she could see. Gail would always be viewed by the world as one of his women. Not his woman. She had to figure out how she felt about that and if she was strong enough to go into a relationship with him anyway.

"You made that clear when you left. But I'm not about to let you go home in a cab when I have a car."

"I'm being difficult, aren't I?" she asked at last.

"A little," he said.

"It's my nature. You asked me if I was scared of you earlier, and I said no. I'm really not. But I am a little unsure of myself because you tempt me to forget common sense, and I'm not about to do that."

"When the time is right, we'll figure it out. Until then, I'll have to woo you. But don't forget, I'm playing to win."

It was all she thought about. That and the fact that, if he

won, she didn't want to be the loser. She didn't want to be standing alone at the end of these matchmaking dates with a handful of memories and a broken heart. She wouldn't allow it.

"I heard that the first time. I think you shouldn't view relationships as something you need to win," she said.

"Why not?" he asked. He seemed to genuinely want to make this work, and she felt bad that she was putting up obstacles.

"Because then you make everything into a best-of competition, that's not a way to build something."

"I'll consider what you said. There's my driver. Good night, Gail."

"Good night, Russell," she said, walking away from him, wishing she could dismiss him from her mind as easily.

Russell spent the morning in meetings and the afternoon doing some promo spots for the show. He'd hoped to see Gail, but it was just Willow and a cameraman following him around the hotel to show him in his everyday world. When shooting wrapped for the day, he pulled Willow aside.

"Do you have time to join me for a drink?"

"I have about fifteen minutes," she said.

"Good." He led her to the VIP section of the bar, which was empty at this time of the day. Russell signaled one of the waitresses to bring them some drinks.

"What did you want to talk about? Gail already called and said she'd be continuing on the show."

"I assumed she had, or you wouldn't be here now," Russell said. "I wanted to ask you about Gail."

"I don't know what I can tell you," Willow said, shaking her long hair. She reminded him a little of Cher back in her younger days, before she was famous on her own. Willow had impressed him as being very smart and tenacious in getting what she wanted.

"She's so guarded, and you two are friends, right?" Russell asked. He'd seen the way they were together and was asking just to hear her confirm it.

"She's one of my best friends. And she is guarded. What do you want to know?" Willow asked. The waitress stopped by, and Willow ordered a Diet Coke and Russell asked for Perrier.

At night, this bar was jam-packed with people. It had rich, dark carpet with an abstract design. The VIP area was lined with banquettes where A-listers could sit obscured from view from but still seeing everything that was happening. It was a world and an environment he knew well, and Willow looked out of place in her jeans and T-shirt. Russell suspected Gail wouldn't be that comfortable here either.

As soon as the waitress left, Russell turned back to Willow. "I want to know…everything. But that's not going to happen, is it?"

"No. If she wants you to know something, she'll tell you," Willow said. "I don't think I can be of much help."

"She's different, Willow. I want to know the best way to get her to open up to me. If she stays guarded…well, neither of us is going to get what we wanted from the matchmaking."

The waitress dropped off their drinks, and Willow took a long sip of hers. "You have to get her to relax. In your case, I'd say she's going to have to forget all the stuff she's heard about you over the years, and that's going to be hard. But once she starts seeing the real you, she'll drop her guard."

"Okay," he said. He had no idea who the real Russell

was. He'd spent so much time pretending to be whatever was needed to make money and be successful, Russell the man had gotten lost. But did that really matter? He didn't need to know who he was to woo Gail. He needed to know what Gail was looking for on her mythical Mr. Right list. "Thanks for that."

"I suspect you already knew that," Willow said.

"I did. I was hoping you'd say jewels or expensive presents would help."

Willow laughed. "That would be easier, wouldn't it? But she has her own money and doesn't really need *things*."

"What *does* she need?" he asked. "Do you know what is on her list of qualities for a man?"

"That's the million-dollar question," Willow said. "She's not open about that, even with her friends."

That was very interesting. So this list of hers was highly personal. It reassured him that she wasn't out talking about it with anyone. He was going to have to get her to trust him completely to find out what was in her heart and soul. And he instinctively knew he'd need to win both to convince the world that he'd changed.

"How long have you known each other?" Russell asked.

"Since grade school," Willow said, leaning back in her chair and smiling. "We grew up together."

"Wow, that's a long time. Most people don't tend to keep in touch over the years. I guess friendship is important to you both," Russell said.

"It is. We've always been close, and it's harder to maintain that relationship as we've gotten older, but we try," Willow said.

"That's good. I don't really…" Russell didn't know why he'd allowed the conversation to go down this path. He didn't want to talk about his growing-up years. In fact, most days he just ignored them.

"You don't have friends from your childhood?" Willow asked.

He thought about the isolated ranch he'd grown up on in New Zealand and the small town where everyone had known his story. His parents had died in a fiery car crash when he was sixteen. He'd been old enough to be considered a man and had started supporting himself by playing cards. He'd always been lucky, and he'd turned that luck at the table into the basis of his fortune.

He hadn't had friends and hadn't looked for them. He'd always wanted so much more than that place had to offer, and leaving it behind had been very easy to do.

"Not really. I'm not into that. I'm always looking for the next business goal," Russell said.

"Is that what you're doing now?" Willow asked. She was very direct and stared into his eyes when she asked him a question.

Russell had been looking at Gail from the angle of what she could do for him and his business. He'd known it all along, but there was no way he could admit to that now.

"I'm looking for a change. Maybe I want a little of that commitment you all have," he said.

She arched both eyebrows at him, and he had the feeling that if he crossed her, he'd be in big trouble.

"Is that what you said to Gail to convince her to stay on the show?" she asked.

"Didn't she tell you?" He was trying to piece together the woman that Gail was. Did she share the intimate details of her life with her closest friends? Or did she keep secrets?

"Actually, no, she didn't elaborate," Willow said, giving him a hard stare.

"Then I won't either. Thank you for your time, Willow," Russell said.

"You're welcome," she said, standing up and stretching. Willow didn't look anything like Gail, and he wondered at the bond of their friendship. In his experience, women tended to surround themselves with similar types. But these two didn't seem to have anything in common.

Russell walked her back to the front of the hotel. As he said goodbye, Willow turned abruptly and poked one finger into the center of his chest, forcing him to back up.

"Don't hurt my friend," she warned.

"I don't intend to," he said. He wanted Gail happier than she'd ever been before, because that was the only way he was going to know that he'd won her over. And winning was all that mattered now.

When Willow left, he stood there in the middle of the Kiwi Klub's hotel lobby, watching the people come and go around him. He'd worked hard to be successful, and it was apparent to him that he'd achieved what he'd set out to do. And he knew that he'd achieve what he wanted with Gail, because he wasn't a man who accepted failure.

He had his eye on the ball, and it wasn't just one goal he had in mind. He was going to convince the head of the Family Vacation Destination company to sell their controlling shares to him. He was going to make damned sure that Gail understood he wasn't playing around with her. It was time for him to move into the next phase in his life, and she was just the woman to help him do it.

Five

Gail didn't question her desire to know every detail about Russell Holloway, but when she found herself running a Google search on him for the fourth time in a single morning, she knew she needed to call him.

She took a sip of her Earl Grey tea and leaned back in the chair. She wanted to find answers easily, some sort of information that would make her feel safer about dating Russell. But the truth was there wasn't anything on the internet that could do that.

She wasn't going to find the information she wanted by reading articles about his childhood in New Zealand or when he'd made his first billion with the Kiwi Klubs. She wanted…what, exactly?

She knew but she just didn't want to admit it. She wanted to hear his story from his mouth. So without overanalyzing it any further, she picked up the phone and dialed his number.

"Holloway," he said, answering his phone on the first ring. His voice was strong and all business. She almost hung up, but she hadn't called him for nothing.

"It's Gail," she said, feeling nervous all of a sudden and a little shy.

There was a pause on the line, and Gail had second thoughts. Oh, this had bad idea written all over it.

"Well, hello, beautiful," he said, his voice softening and the charm she remembered from their first date returning.

"Beautiful?" she said.

"To me you are."

Gail knew she wasn't in the same league as Penny, so she dismissed his compliment. He seemed to be the kind of man who used endearments for everyone.

"I have some questions for you."

"Shoot," he said. "I'm an open book."

"Yeah, right."

She wanted to see his face when she talked to him about his past. There was a lot about him she didn't know, and she was tired of her fruitless searches. Who was the real Russell? "I was hoping we could meet and talk in person."

"I'm booked all afternoon, and have a VIP coming in tonight that I can't pawn off on my duty manager."

She smiled to herself. This was one match between them that she was going to win. "You're a workaholic. That is not on my list of qualities in Mr. Right. I'm going to have to make a note of that."

"Well played. I can give you ten minutes, but it has to be at the Club," he said.

"I'll be right there," she said.

"Text me when you get here," he said.

"I will. Thanks, Russell," she said, preparing to hang up the phone.

"You owe me one, beautiful," he said in that deep, husky voice of his.

"Stop calling me that," she said, even though she liked the sound of it. Endearments and compliments made her uncomfortable. She didn't think of herself in those terms, and hearing him say it... "Are you mocking me?"

"When?" he asked.

God, why had she started asking him about this? She didn't want to discuss her lack of attractiveness with one of *People*'s Sexiest Bachelors.

"When you call me beautiful," she said at last, hoping her voice didn't sound as small and vulnerable as she felt.

"No, I'm not," he said. "Why do you think that?"

"No reason," she said. She should have learned her lesson a long time ago, she thought, about keeping her thoughts to herself. "I'll see you in a few minutes."

She disconnected before he could say anything else. She should have kept her insecurity to herself, but she didn't know how to do the dating thing and pretend to be someone she wasn't. In PR it was different, because she knew the rules and scripted what others said. But for herself, always shot from the hip and spoke from the heart.

She left her office and headed for the Kiwi Klub. When she got there, she texted Russell but didn't have to wait in the cutting-edge lobby long for him to show up. He walked toward her in a pair of casual slacks and a button-down shirt, left open at the collar. He was talking to a slim man with thick hair and glasses, but the man left as Russell approached her.

"Hello, Gail. So nice to see you again," he said, putting his arm around her and giving her a small hug.

"Hello, Russell," she said, hugging him back and pretending that this was normal for her. But it had been a long time since she'd been so comfortable with a man that they exchanged hugs.

"We can go to my office to chat," he said, leading the way.

"Sounds good. I'm sorry for the short notice, but I was doing some internet research on you—

"Man, I hate Google. No privacy at all anymore," he said, stopping to hold open a door to a hallway marked Private.

"True enough for people who are in the public eye. I have relatively little info that isn't work related on there," she said. She felt smug about her totally gossip-free life for a moment, but then remembered that it could also come off as somewhat boring.

"That's not true. I found some pictures of you from high school," he said.

She blushed, remembering her big glasses and how she'd looked back then. "How on earth did you find them?"

Russell shrugged one shoulder. "I have my ways. Here's my office."

The office was luxurious by anyone's standards, with a big walnut desk dominating the center of the room and dark paneling on the walls. Hanging at different points around the room were photos of Russell with various celebrities.

"Have a seat," he said, gesturing to the leather guest chairs.

She took her time walking to one of them and then sat down, surprised when Russell sat in the one next to her. Now that she was here, what was she going to say? In her head she'd had the idea that if they were face-to-face, she'd be able to see past the facade of his reputation to the real man—especially without the cameras rolling—but right now she wasn't sure.

"I…I sort of had a plan, but I'm not sure I can ask you the questions I wanted to," she said.

"Why not?" he asked.

"Because they're intrusive," she said. When she wasn't with Russell, it was easier for her to think of him as an object. As someone that she could ask personal questions of and not worry about how he felt. But now, sitting across from him, she realized how nosey she was being.

"Ask away. I'm planning to do the same to you."

"You are?" She had figured that he wouldn't be that worried about her. She didn't have a reputation at all, except in her professional life as someone who got the job done. "But I'm the normal one."

He laughed at that. "Good to know how you're thinking of me."

"I didn't mean it that way. Just that I'm the one who you'd expect to see on a dating show. You aren't."

He leaned back in his chair and casually sprawled his legs out in front of him. He was a tall man, long and lean, and she was distracted by him. "I'm counting on you to help me seem like a man who is moving on. I can't be that if you have skeletons in your closet."

She didn't have anything controversial in her past, so that didn't bother her. And hearing him say he had doubts about her was oddly reassuring. It made him real to her in a way that all the questions in the world wouldn't have.

"Fair enough, I guess," she said, wondering what kind of questions he would have for her. "You can go first."

He shook his index finger at her. "No way. That's not how this works. You called me and demanded this meeting."

"Fine," she said, sighing. Then she mentally reviewed

the questions she wanted answered. Most of them involved his past relationships. She wanted to try to find a pattern in how he'd behaved, so she'd have an idea of what to expect from him.

"Why did you settle that paternity suit?" she asked.

"Which one?" he asked.

Though he didn't move, he no longer appeared relaxed. After a moment he leaned forward and laced his fingers together.

"Was there more than one?"

"Yes. I've settled three. I'm going to tell you something that I won't discuss in public or with you after this...."

"Okay," she said. Three paternity suits—wow. That was more than she'd expected. And she really didn't know what to make of that information. Did that mean that he didn't want children?

"I am not the father of any of those children, but the women were all friends of mine who needed a hand. I have a reputation as a player and enough money to take care of all my needs."

"So you just helped them out?" she asked.

"I did," he said.

"Why would you do that? Were the kids yours but you just didn't want to be a dad?" she asked. "I'd think you'd want to clear your name and move on."

He shrugged and looked away from her. "The first case was a girl I'd grown up with and I'm not really sure how it happened—maybe a slow news week or something, but the story made headlines and the longer I played it out the more customers we had at the Kiwi Klubs. So I let it go on and then settled it. The press lapped it up and the new customers I'd found stayed."

"So it was just a press stunt?" she asked. She should

have expected that. Wasn't that the way most of her clients would have reacted?

"It became that, but my intent was to just handle it and move on," he said.

"What about the kids?" she asked. "Do you see them?"

"No. They know I'm not their dad. I don't talk about them or the situation ever," he said.

"I don't like this," she said.

"I can't change it," he said. "Would you rather I lied and made up some sweet story about always wanting kids so I helped out to get to know the babies?"

She shook her head and glanced down at her lap. But, yes, she would have preferred that. She was starting to like Russell, but this…this didn't jibe with her image of what Mr. Right should be.

"Liar," he said, not unkindly.

"Sorry, you're right. I do want you to have acted for a different reason," she admitted.

"Is that on your Mr. Right list?"

"No. I don't want a man with kids. I have a friend who's divorced with kids and every guy she dates has a problem with the kids. I think it's a complication I don't need."

"You're trying to make this match based on an image rather than what it really is. No one is going to be as perfect as the Mr. Right in your head," he said. "I'm not going to lie to you about this. It's easier for me to let the media and the public think I'm shallow."

"You are shallow," she said.

"Am I? Don't just assume everything I do is for my own pleasure."

"Isn't it?" she asked, questioning what she knew about him. He was saying one thing, but a part of her wondered if there wasn't more to his settling paternity suits than he'd let on.

He arched one eyebrow at her. "I think I've answered that. My turn to ask you a question," he said, leveling that cool gray gaze on her.

She had no secrets, the way he did, so she didn't know why she was so concerned about what he would ask. Except that she didn't want to let him really get to know her until she was sure about him. She wanted to protect herself and her heart, but after his honesty, she couldn't lie.

Russell was glad that Gail had asked to see him today. He wanted to know more about her, but wouldn't have pursued the information this way. Not the way she had. But thanks to her curiosity, he now had carte blanche to find out whatever he wanted.

This was the only time they'd had together that wasn't part of the television show or setup dates. She looked professional and polished, but not the way she had on the show. Her hair was pulled back, revealing her long neck and her high cheek bones.

He couldn't stop looking at her. This was the real woman, he thought. She wore a sundress belted at the waist and looked very Hamptons casual to him. She was successful and wore the trappings of it well. No other woman he'd ever dated had pulled off the look that she had right now. She was…well, understated and sophisticated, and he could easily see her on his arm at a business dinner or as his hostess at a party.

"What do you want to know about me?" she asked, her voice low and husky as she waited for him.

He really didn't think she had any skeletons, but his questions were all very personal and intimate. "Do you like for a man to seduce you slowly?"

She blushed and shook her head. "I should have known you would ask something about sex."

"You should have. I'm attracted to you, Gail, and I intend to have you soon."

Her eyes widened as she looked at him. "I like a slow seduction that gives me time to get in the mood. I've never had a lover who could turn me on with just one touch or one look."

He intended to change that. He wanted to be the man who knew her well enough to push her buttons effortlessly, because she already did that for him.

"Have you?" she asked.

That question caught him off guard. He'd kind of expected her to retreat when he turned the conversation to more intimate matters, but then Gail had yet to react the way he'd thought she would to anything. "When I was a teenager, a girl just had to bump into me to turn me on, but as an adult with my hormones under control...no, no woman has been able to turn me on with just a glance."

"Interesting," she said. "Do you think it's because we both use barriers to keep others at bay?"

"Probably," he said. "I didn't think you'd admit to the barriers."

"Why not?" she asked. "I know better than anyone that I don't like to let people too close. I've always been this way."

"Why do you think that is?"

She shrugged as if she didn't know the answer, but in her eyes, he saw the evidence that she was very aware of why she did it. She wasn't interested in sharing her deepest, darkest secrets. She kept them hidden for a reason.

"Tell me," he said.

"It's not something I want to share this early in a relationship," she said and turned away from him. He could see that she didn't want to expose herself to him. It was one thing to pry into his life—he was in the gossip magazines—but she was just a normal, average girl with her own fears. "It's too private."

He almost let her have her way, but he was in this to win, and he knew he'd never win Gail over if he let her set the terms and boundaries of whatever developed between them. "Asking me about the paternity suits wasn't?"

"Touché," she said. "Somehow it felt different because your business is all out there, you know?"

"I can see how it would seem that way, but it's still personal."

She nodded and shifted so she was facing him. "My parents had a very nasty divorce when I was eight. I know it doesn't sound traumatic, but each of them would watch me for any little upset and blame the other one for my sadness. Eventually, I just learned to keep all my emotions bottled up. And then that turned into keeping people at arm's length."

"How does that translate to keeping your distance?"

"My dad gave me everything I wanted, and my friends were aware of that. I had a lot of people start hanging out with me to get whatever they could. That's one reason why Willow and I are such good friends. She didn't care about the parties or the stuff—she just liked hanging out with me."

"Early on you learned to trust your gut," he said. "Willow is a good friend and she's earned your trust."

"Yes, she has."

"I intend to do the same thing, Gail. I don't need your money, and I'm not going to use your emotions against you," he said. But he felt a twinge as he acknowledged to himself that he needed her to fall in love with him so that he could convince the public he'd changed. Gail wasn't the kind of woman who would ever pretend convincingly that she loved a man. He'd have to win her over, heart and soul, and that was exactly what he intended to do.

But he promised himself he'd give her the world. Make sure she had everything she wanted, and he wondered if her father had perhaps told himself the same thing when he was vying with Gail's mother for her affection.

"Why are you looking at me like that?" she asked.

"I just don't want to be another reason why you keep people away," he said. "I want to be the reason why you look at life with new eyes, beautiful. And I'm not going to be satisfied until I'm convinced that you do."

Gail had never intended to tell Russell about her parents, but she felt that it was important to keep things even between them. Her sense of fairness was deeply ingrained, and she just couldn't shift away from it.

"I won't let you be a reason for me to keep people at bay," she said. "That's why I went to the matchmaker."

"There is still no guarantee," he said.

"Are you trying to tell me you are using me?" she asked. "I think you're very good at reading what people want."

"No, I'm not using you. I can read a man when he sits down across from me in the boardroom or at a poker table, but I can only see if he is hiding something. Women are different…unpredictable."

She looked askance at him. "Only a man would say that."

"Damned straight," he said. "Women think they are so easy to understand."

"We know we are complicated," she said, with a grin. "We just think that men should get that and not be afraid of the challenge."

"I'll do my best. Do you have any more questions for me?" he asked.

"Have you heard any more from Penny?" she asked. The starlet had been quiet since their encounter the other night, but since she was a part of Russell's past, Gail didn't want to ignore her.

"Not yet. Don't worry about Penny. She is definitely part of my past. And you, Gail, are my future," he said.

She felt a little thrill go through her. She'd never been called that before, and even though she suspected he was saying it to make her believe they would have a successful match, she wanted to believe it. She wanted a man who said the right things and turned on the charm with her. Russell was very good at that.

"Well, I hope she knows that, "Gail said.

"She does," Russell said. "Stand up for a minute."

"Why?" she asked, suddenly not too sure of herself.

"Something you said earlier is bothering me," he said.

"What?" He made her feel…just made her feel more alive and, conversely, more insecure than she ever had before.

"Stand up and I'll tell you," he said, rising and holding out his hand to her.

She took his hand and allowed him to draw her to her feet. He led her to the corner of his office, where a large gilt-framed mirror hung over an antique credenza. He stood behind her, and she saw how inadequate she looked on his arm. Whereas Penny looked like the perfect little Barbie to his Ken, she looked like…Barbie's less glamorous, generic cousin.

She tried to turn away but Russell enfolded her in his arms from behind. She liked the feeling of being surrounded by him. She leaned her head back against his shoulder and stared up at him.

"Look in the mirror, Gail," he said.

"I don't want to," she said, shaking her head and looking down.

"Why not?" he asked, taking her chin in his hand and tracing the curve of her jaw, then slowly caressing her neck and shoulder bones.

"We don't look like we belong together," she said.

"That's the problem," he said, leaning down to kiss her so softly that she thought she might have imagined it.

"Look again and let me tell you what I see," he said, his tone so inviting that she was tempted to do just what he asked.

She swallowed hard and then turned to look at them in the mirror. She loved the way his gray eyes were so sincere as he looked at her. And she wondered how she could have thought he was shallow. He had more substance than most men she'd met, and she realized how hard he must work to keep up that image.

"See how perfectly we fit together," he said. "I have thought of nothing else but how it will feel when we make love. You feel just right in my arms."

"You do fit me just right," she said. "You're not too tall, and when I kissed you…your mouth was…you tasted good."

He smiled at her in the mirror, and she didn't feel as awkward as she had a few minutes ago.

"Your eyes are big, bottomless pools of dark chocolate that I get lost in," he said.

"Even with the glasses?" she asked.

"Especially then," he said. He pushed her glasses up on the top of her head and rubbed the bridge of her nose, then drew his fingertip down to her lips, where he traced the outline of her mouth before putting her glasses back on.

"When I look at you, I see the most beautiful woman in

the world. The only woman I want and the woman I need by my side. I know that we are just beginning this relationship, but already I feel like you belong to me."

She had no answer for that and she wished she did. But she looked at them again in the mirror and then felt his hands loosen the pins in her hair until it fell around her shoulders in long, curly waves.

"Gorgeous. Why would you wear your hair any other way?" he asked. "You have a natural beauty that other women would kill for."

She shook her head, feeling the soft weight of her hair on her shoulders. She wanted to believe him when he looked at her hair, but she'd spent her life in a straight, smooth hairstyle world, and she knew that this crazy mass of curls didn't fit in. "My hair is a big frizz, but I'm glad you like it."

He pinched her side lightly. "Why won't you just believe that you are gorgeous? You have to get that negative self-image out of your head. You are beautiful, Gail, and before long I'm going to have you believing it too."

"I…I hope you can do that, Russell, but it is going to be hard," she said. Her entire life she'd felt too big, too curly, too dark to really fit in with the popular, beautiful girls. It didn't matter that she'd gotten out in the world and become successful—her inner mirror was always dialed to that look that she knew she'd never be able to achieve.

He turned her in his arms, his hands cupping her face. "I will not be satisfied until I've gotten you to see yourself as I see you."

She couldn't really think as he lowered his head and kissed her. It wasn't a tentative first embrace, as the previous kisses had been. This was the kiss of a lover intent on having his woman. And she could do nothing but surrender to him. She needed this from him. She wanted him.

Her skin felt sensitized and her breasts suddenly felt fuller. She leaned in so that she could rub them against his chest. His hands slid down her back to her waist, and he held her closer to him.

She leaned into him and forgot to breathe, losing herself in a swirl of sensations that centered around Russell's body and his mouth moving over hers. She knew that this was dangerous, because he was finding chinks in the wall she'd always used to protect herself, but she couldn't help it. He was more than she'd expected to find in any real man, and she felt herself starting to fall.

Six

Russell didn't want to stop kissing Gail. She felt more than right in his arms. He knew with a gut-deep instinct that this was the one place where he felt the most comfortable being honest. It didn't matter that he had business goals he needed her help to achieve. Even if all that disappeared, he'd still want Gail.

Her waist was tiny; he was able to span it with his hands and lift her more fully into his body. Her full breasts brushed against his chest as he lifted her onto the credenza. He kept his mouth moving over hers.

He pushed one thigh between her legs and felt her shift as her legs parted for him. He moved closer as her hands slid up and down his back, drawing him in. His blood ran heavier in his veins as he hardened for her.

Her touch was light and sure as she reached lower to cup his buttocks and draw him in even closer. He inched her skirt up her thighs, feeling the muscled smoothness of her legs.

The knock on the door startled him, and he drew back, pulling his mouth from hers. She started as well, her eyes going wide, but her pupils were dilated with the onset of lust and her lips were wet and swollen. He cussed under his breath.

"Who is it?" he barked toward the door.

"Dylan needs you in the lobby, Russell," Mitsy, his assistant, said through the door.

"Dammit," he said under his breath, but he stepped away from the credenza and helped Gail off it. He didn't want to go. He wanted to stay here in this office with the door shut and this woman in his arms. "I'll be right there."

"Wow. That got out of control," she said. She reached for her hair and started to pull it back into the tight bun she'd had it in earlier. Her lips were swollen and her pupils were still dilated with passion.

To his way of thinking, it hadn't gotten nearly as far out of control as he would have liked. "Leave your hair down. It's incredible."

She nodded and left it hanging around her shoulders. The curls were thick and soft, and he reached for her before realizing he couldn't kiss her or hold her right now. He had to go take care of the situation in the lobby.

"Will you have dinner with me tonight?" he asked. "I can't wait to see you again."

"I've got tickets for the basketball game," she said. "Want to join me?"

Basketball wasn't his thing, but Gail was, so he'd make the sacrifice. In fact, he thought that the corporation had a box at Madison Square Garden. "Yes. I'll pick you up."

"Sounds good," she said. "I never intended for that to happen. For you to kiss me like that."

He laughed. "I did."

She just shook her head at him. "I'm sure you did. Made me forget all the things I wanted to say."

"Good. You talk a lot," he said. But he liked it. She didn't sulk in silence. Instead, she just said what was on her mind. It was a different experience for him.

"Too much?" she asked, playfully.

"Not at all," he assured her.

He led the way past his assistant, and for the first time outside of the business world, he felt a sense of peace. That wasn't the right word exactly, but he was at home where he was with the person next to him. From the first moment he'd seen her, he'd known Gail was different, but now he was realizing just how much.

"I'll see you out," he said.

"I can take care of myself," she said.

"I have no doubt about that," he said. "But I like doing things for you, Gail."

"But you have to go take care of your business."

"Okay. Let me know what time to pick you up tonight," he said. Then he remembered he was hosting a dinner for the Family Vacation Destination hotel group. "Oh, hell, I just remembered I have a VIP event tonight. I can't make it to the game."

"I remember you mentioning it now," she said with a shy grin. "I forgot in your office."

"Me too. All I could think about was you. You go to my head."

"You do the same to me," she said.

"How about I stop by for a nightcap when I'm done?" he suggested. He hoped she'd say yes, but had no idea if she would.

"Okay. Just text me when you're done." Gail felt a little giddy at how well coming to see Russell had turned out.

She was feeling better and better about matchmaking. But all of that changed when she stepped out of the back office and saw who was waiting for Russell in the lobby—Penny Thomson. Just like that, Gail was reminded that the man she thought was being honest with her had a long track record of dealing with the opposite sex, and he had learned more than one trick.

"We need to talk," Penny said, as soon as she saw him enter the lobby. His grip on Gail's arm tightened.

"In a minute," Russell said. "Gail, are we still on?"

"You really don't want to keep me waiting, Russ. I have news, and I'm tired of you playing with me," Penny said.

Gail didn't like the way the other woman was talking to Russell, but she wasn't going to interfere. "Call me later."

"I will," he said.

Gail walked away, though she wanted to stay and see what was going on and how Russell was going to handle his ex-girlfriend. Given what he'd told her and his history with women, the situation was going to probably be a big PR nightmare. And Gail was going to be dragged into it.

She hailed a cab as the entire afternoon swirled in her mind. The quiet, sharing conversation they'd had. The kiss that had made her want to believe everything he'd said. And then there was his ex-girlfriend. What was Gail going to do? She felt as if, from the moment she'd signed up with Matchmakers Inc., nothing was under her control.

The drive to her office felt longer than it ever had before. She didn't know what she wanted anymore. She knew that this matchmaking wasn't going to work out. And she had so craved that family she'd had in her head. That picture-perfect image that it seemed fate didn't have in store for her. It hadn't been hers as a child, nor would it be as an adult. Maybe if she was lucky Willow and Nichole would have children some day and she could be their auntie and spoil them.

The cabbie pulled to a stop in front of her building and she got out after paying him. She hated giving up on her dream, but she knew better than to keep pursuing something when it was clear that it was a losing prospect. And she knew that she was giving up on more than just her dream of a family—she was also giving up on Russell.

Russell was beyond over Penny. But he knew that he couldn't just keep pushing her away. As soon as they were out of view of the public, he took her wrist in his hand and drew her to a stop.

"Never speak to Gail like that again," he said, warning her for the last time. He'd put up with a lot of bad behavior from Penny, but he wasn't about to let her interfere with what he had with Gail.

"Is that her name?" Penny asked, tossing her blond hair around her shoulders. "She seems like a nice girl, Russell, not your normal type of woman."

"You've got that right," he said. She was different and that's why he needed her. But this afternoon, he hadn't been thinking about all the reasons he needed to change his reputation.

"Maybe I should warn her of the kind of man you are. How you use up everything a woman has to give and then you just move on," Penny said.

"I didn't use you up. You dumped me, remember?" he asked. "You were the one who was ready to move on to someone more Hollywood."

"Semantics. You were ready to move on, you just didn't want to say it first," she said.

Russell knew that was true, but he would never have

dumped Penny. She was fun and had, until this moment, been someone he truly liked. "What happened, Penny?"

"I told you before. I'm pregnant. The baby is yours, and you're going to have to do your duty by me," she said.

"Did you arrange for the paternity test?" he asked. He knew the results would reveal he wasn't the father. He was infertile, but that wasn't something that any women knew. He'd kept that close to the chest, knowing that virility in a man was still prized in this day and age.

"No. As soon as I do that, you know it will show up on the news. We should handle this between us," she said, then turned those big blue eyes up at him. "Come on, baby, just do the right thing here."

"If you're honest with me, I'll do whatever I can to help you," he said. And he wasn't lying. He wanted to help her out in any way he could.

Indecision flitted across Penny's face, and for a moment he thought that maybe he could get her to talk sensibly to him.

Then she shook her head. "I am being honest. You're the one with something to hide."

"From who? I'm not hiding anything," Russell said. As much as he wanted not to be faced with another paternity suit, he wasn't going to be blackmailed by Penny.

"Gail, isn't that her name? She's not going to want to be in a relationship with a man who has your kind of drama."

"I don't have any drama. I have an ex-girlfriend who has trouble letting go," Russell said.

"Russ, I'm asking you to just give me the money I need and I'll walk away."

Russell wondered what was going on with Penny and made a mental note to investigate. "Do you need money?"

"Never mind," she said, looking away from him. "I can't talk to you when you're being difficult. I'm scheduled to be on Jimmy Fallon tonight—if I haven't heard from you before then, I will be breaking the news of my pregnancy."

"Penny, it's not my baby," he said.

"I don't see it that way. And the world will definitely believe me, Russ," she said. "You have my number."

She walked out, and Russell turned and punched the wall. He wasn't going to let her get away with manipulating him like that. But he knew Penny well enough to guess she wasn't bluffing. If she said she was going to tell the viewing public he was the father of her unborn child tonight, then she'd go through with it.

He also wasn't going to be able to keep Gail in the dark. Suddenly the VIP guest he had coming into the hotel tonight didn't matter. He needed to sort out his personal life, and he had to do it now.

He knew that Gail was going to the basketball game, and called the concierge to find out what time the game started. Then he called his assistant in.

"Get me Dylan. Cancel all my appointments for the afternoon and try to get Gail Little back here. I'm going to be on the phone," Russell said to his assistant Mitsy as he walked into his office.

"Yes, sir." Mitsy sat at a desk that had two computers on it and more gadgets than most people would be comfortable handling. She was the hub of his international business and went with him wherever he traveled. She had no life outside of working for him and freely admitted she was happy that way.

Russell approached this latest problem with the same calmness he faced all adversity. He wasn't about to let Penny throw off his plans for the future of his Kiwi Klubs or for Gail. When Dylan arrived, they discussed the evening's VIPs and what needed to be done. Then he called his PR agent, but he knew he was going to need Gail at his side.

As Russell was headed to the game, the concierge got back to him with the information on the Kiwi Klub's corporate booth. Mitsy hadn't managed to get in touch with Gail, so Russell was left with trying to find her at Madison Square Garden during a basketball game. Not an easy prospect, but he had a connection at the Garden and paid for a message to be played on the JumboTron. So he wasn't surprised when, shortly after his message ran, his cell phone rang and it was Gail.

"You wanted me to call you?" she said.

"Yes. Can you meet me in my suite? I have to talk to you and it couldn't wait," he said. This was not the way he usually handled this sort of thing, but he felt that he had no choice. The last thing he wanted was for Gail to hear about Penny's claims on late-night television.

"I…I thought you weren't going to be able to come to the game," she said.

"Circumstances changed. Please join me," he implored, using his most persuasive voice.

"I'm on my way," he thought he heard her say, though it was hard to hear her in the crowd. "Is something wrong?"

Russell knew he didn't want to discuss Penny on the phone with her. But lying wasn't an option either. "I don't think it's going to be a big problem, but I need to talk to you in person."

"Hmm…that's not the no I was hoping for. I'm on the elevator to your suite. I'll be there in a minute," she said. "I hope this isn't going to interfere with me watching the game."

"Thank you for coming up here," he said. "I'm sorry to say, I think it will definitely tinge your game watching tonight."

"No problem. The least I can do is listen to whatever you have to say after you answered all of my questions this afternoon. I was teasing about the game," she said, disconnecting the call.

Russell looked around the corporate suite. It was fully stocked and set to his specifications. His favorite scotch was at the bar, and he went over to pour himself a drink.

The door behind him opened, and he glanced over his shoulder to see Gail standing there in a pair of skintight jeans and a slim-fitting Knicks jersey. Her thick hair was up in a ponytail, and she looked good to him.

This moment made him realize that he didn't want to let her slip away, and he knew without a doubt that the problems with Penny were jeopardizing his future with Gail.

She knew as soon as she saw him that there was a problem. He had the same look in his eyes that her celebrity clients had when they'd been caught doing something they shouldn't. She put aside her thought that he was here for a date and realized that he must need her professional help.

"What's up?" she asked, trying not to worry, even though the last time she'd seen him, his ex-girlfriend had been with him and it hadn't seemed that she was just dropping by to catch up.

"Let me get you a drink first," he said, going to the wet bar and taking down a highball glass.

"Am I going to need one?" she asked, half joking. Russell was serious, not the playful lover he'd been in his office earlier, and she wondered what exactly the problem was today.

"I don't think so. But what would you like?" he asked, holding the empty glass up.

"Perrier, no ice, but a twist of lime," she said. She watched as he made her drink.

"Tell me what's going on," she said.

Russell brought her drink to her and then gestured toward the leather sofa that faced the windows overlooking the court. She took a seat and waited for him to sit down next to her.

"I mentioned earlier that Penny was being a little dramatic about our breakup, and she's taking it to another level tonight," Russell said.

"I don't know why that concerns me," Gail said. "We've only been on one date, and I know I was asking you about her, but it's fine with me—

"She's going to tell a late-night talk-show host that she's pregnant on his show tonight, and that I'm the father," Russell said.

"Oh, well. Is that true?" Gail asked. She'd known. Hadn't she had that feeling in her gut that things weren't going to work out the way she wanted them to?

"No, it's not true," Russell said. "I just felt you should hear it from me instead of the news."

"Thank you," she said, taking a sip of the Perrier. The fizzy drink was soothing, but right now there was nothing that could calm her racing mind. She wanted to know more, to demand that Russell explain to her why Penny was telling the world something that he said wasn't true. But she also knew that this was the excuse she'd been looking for to get away from Russell. To retreat back into her private, safe little world.

"What are you going to do to counter her claim?" she asked. Why was he so confident he wasn't the father? She'd have to ask him about that later.

"Nothing. The last thing I want to do is get into a mud-slinging match with her. I don't have to defend myself to the public," he said.

"That's not the best idea. I think we should call Willow

and let her know as well. She'll want to use the controversy around you to promote the show," Gail said. And just like that, Russell went from being a potential mate to a client. She knew how to handle this problem for him, and it would make him safer to be around. She could manage his PR nightmare and "date" him on the show without letting him get too close.

"I really don't want to do anything about it," he said at last.

"You are going to have to. You said you went to the matchmaker to find a mate and move into a new phase of your life. You can't do that with Penny saying you're a jerk. That isn't going to help things," Gail said. She was also thinking of herself and of the show. This could affect all of them, and they couldn't just let it ride.

Russell swallowed what was left of his scotch, then rubbed the back of his neck. "I don't want this to affect you and me."

"Too late. It already has," she said. "To be honest, I thought something like this might happen when Penny showed up again."

Gail was making notes in her head of what needed to be done. "I can try to get you on a morning talk show. But I'm going to have to get started on this right now. Have you been working with a PR firm?"

"No, I haven't. Why?" he asked.

"We need to draft a message for you and send out a press release. I think it would be best if you just had one consistent message. What do you think it is?"

"That Penny's lying," Russell said.

Gail laughed out loud. Many of her clients had the same reaction to news they didn't like. They wanted to just issue a statement saying it wasn't true and never discuss it again. But that kind of silence just bred more rumors in the media. "That's not going to work."

She toyed with the situation in her head. "Maybe something along the lines of, when your relationship with Penny ended, you both agreed to go your separate ways, but she's trying to continue... No, that won't work. I think you should say that you—"

"I will say whatever you tell me to, but I don't want this to affect you and me, Gail. You're important to me," Russell said.

Gail knew that. He wouldn't have rushed across town to talk to her if she didn't matter to him. But she saw this as her out. It was her safety release and she was going to take it. She'd had doubts about Russell from the beginning, and using this one event as an excuse was going to let her protect herself.

"We can't continue like nothing happened," Gail said. "We have to stay on the show, because that will help you maintain the semblance of a real relationship and show a better side of you, but that's it."

"That's it?" Russell said, leaning closer to her. "What do you mean, that's it? I hope you don't think that we are over because of this."

"Yes, I do," Gail said.

"No. That is not what is going to happen. We are not going to pretend to date. We are going to really date. And I'm going to manage the problems with Penny the way I have in the past. I'm sorry if you thought I called you up here to do your professional job, but what I really wanted was to be with the woman I can't stop thinking about."

"Oh, really?" she asked, giving him a hard look that would have stopped a lesser man.

"Yes. I hate that anything from my past might hurt you

in any way, and I wanted you to hear from my lips that there is nothing to her claims," Russell said.

Gail stared at him, torn between what she knew with her mind and what she wanted with her heart. It was hard, because she liked Russell. He was no longer just some tabloid playboy, but a real man to her. She wanted to believe, him but she was afraid.

She'd still try to keep him in her life by agreeing to continue the show. She knew that she was going to be careful when it came to her emotions, but she was not going to let him walk away from her. She needed him.

She liked the way he made her feel, and she had seen a different woman in the mirror this evening when she was getting ready. She was starting to see herself through Russell's eyes.

"Okay I'll try my best, but I think you're going to have a hard time managing this without releasing a statement. I don't think I should be repping you, because that doesn't seem right."

"Fine, I'll do whatever you suggest, as long as you continue to give the matchmaking and our dates your real devotion," he said.

"I will," she said. "Will you?"

"Hell, yes. Starting right now. Thanks to Penny, we get to have dinner together and watch the game."

"We do?" she asked.

"Yes," he said. "The executive chef from my restaurant has prepared dinner for us, and the staff here will be serving it during the first quarter."

She nodded, no longer feeling that Russell needed her to manage his PR crisis, but that he was wooing her. What was he up to?

Seven

Russell spent the next three days being kept at arm's length by Gail. She'd send him information for the press releases that the PR firm she'd suggested should use. And she couldn't help but send him recommendations for shows for him to call into, but personally she stayed away. He didn't blame her for wanting to stay out of the maelstrom that was produced by Penny's pronouncement on late-night TV.

Even Willow and Conner had pulled him aside to make sure that he was still going to stay on the matchmaking show. Russell didn't like it, and had sent his lawyers around to Penny to see if they could figure out how to get her to stop going public with everything.

His board of directors weren't too pleased with him either, and Family Vacation Destinations decided to decline his bid for their resorts. As far as his plan to add the launch of a new chain of Kiwi Family Klubs to his existing Kiwi Klubs, he wasn't exactly on track. So he'd called Dylan into his office for a daylong meeting to figure out the business aspect of pushing past the mess Penny had created by telling the world he was a deadbeat dad.

He didn't let himself dwell on the problems with Gail. They had their second taped date this afternoon, and he had a feeling that once they were alone, he would be able to convince her to let go of whatever apprehensions she had.

"The board will come around as soon as they see this quarter's profits, but we need to have the Family Vacation Destinations owners here—we need to show them the improvements we have made at this resort to make it more family friendly."

"I'm on it, boss," Dylan said. "The new kids' zone hires are ready for a meeting with you. Once we have your approval on the events and the budget, we are ready to implement the plan."

"Sounds good. Make sure Mitsy gets that on my calendar for this week. Do we have anything else that I need to handle right now?"

"I think that's it," Dylan said. "Will you be reachable by phone later?"

"I have my second matchmaking date, so my phone will be off for a few hours. I'll check in when I can," Russell said.

"Where will you be?" Dylan asked.

"Montauk Yacht Club."

"Sounds good. I can handle everything here," Dylan said. "I've learned a lot in the last few weeks."

"I know you can do it," Russell said. "You are a good assistant."

"Glad you noticed. I'm planning to ask you for a raise at my next review." Dylan laughed a little as he said it.

"If you get Family Vacations Destinations deal back on track, I'm going to give you a huge bonus."

"I was already motivated, but now I really won't let you down," Dylan said.

Dylan was easy to deal with since he was young and hungry. He wanted to move up the corporate ladder, and the word *no* wasn't part of his vocabulary. To be honest, Russell knew that Dylan would burn out one day, but for now, everything was exactly as he needed it to be.

"I know you won't. Thank you, Dylan."

"No problem, boss," Dylan said as he gathered his papers and left the office. Russell leaned back in his chair and glanced over at the credenza and mirror where he'd watched himself kissing Gail. He'd hated the interruption at the time, but if he'd had a clue that she was going to put so many barriers between them, he would have been damned sure to keep her in his arms then.

Russell changed into casual clothes for an afternoon of sailing. He had arranged for the chopper to take him to the heliport in the Hamptons and had invited Gail to join him. She'd agreed, which he had taken as a positive sign.

Gail was waiting at the helipad on top of the Big Apple Kiwi Klub when he got there. She wore a pair of Bermuda shorts that hit the top of her knees and showed her legs off. Her sleeveless casual shirt was open at the collar. She had on a pair of designer sunglasses, and her hair was left to hang around her shoulders.

He wanted her. He was tired of waiting to make another move until things were just right between them. It wasn't like him to wait. He'd been trying to do whatever he could to please her, and he had a feeling he was failing. But now, more than ever, he needed to get control of the situation and of Gail. He was going to be the only man he could be around her. He was tired of playing a part.

She turned around as he approached and gave him that forced half smile she'd been using since she'd heard about Penny. "Oh, hello, Russell."

"Hello, Gail. You look lovely today."

"Thank you," she said, pushing her sunglasses up on her head. She wore contacts today; he could tell because she wasn't blinking to try to see him.

"You look nice too, but a little tired," she said. "How are you holding up with the media stuff?"

"Fine. It's a little demanding, and I'd rather be working than sending out press releases, but I'm following your advice on this," Russell said. She'd actually been a bit of a godsend, in that without him asking she'd acted as a go-between with the PR firm, leaving Russell free to do his business. It had made him realize what a good partner she was for him.

"You should. I'm very good at what I do," she said.

"I wish you'd stop treating me like a client," Russell said.

"Right now, that's all I can do. I want you to be able to move on and get the past behind you. Then you and I will have this great friendship we can build on," she said.

"That's bull," he said.

"What?"

"You don't want to build on this. You just want to keep me in a nice, neat corner where you don't have to reveal any more of your vulnerabilities. But I have news for you. We both went to the matchmakers for a reason, and that hasn't changed. I'm the man they thought was right for you, and despite the problems I'm dealing with, I think that I'm still the right match for you."

She smiled at him, and it was the first genuine expression he'd seen from her in days. He was glad to see that she still reacted to him when he made the effort. He wanted her. He didn't want to think about problems in the workplace, but instead wanted to focus on those long, tan legs of hers.

"You would say that, because you're all ego," she said.

"Just stating the facts," he said, wrapping an arm around her and hugging her close. She fit perfectly under his shoulder, and he realized that he wasn't going to be able to wait much longer to have her. He craved her touch, and he wasn't going to be satisfied until he had a lot more of it.

The chopper pilot arrived, and they were on their way to the Hamptons in a short while. They didn't talk, but Russell didn't let that bother him, as she kept her hand in his during the entire ride. He knew he'd have to keep being his usual, blunt self if he had any chance of getting her to fall for him. Being meek and letting her set the tone wasn't going to give him what he wanted.

And, though in the back of his mind he wanted to believe that he still just wanted Gail to help out with improving his reputation, he knew that he really just wanted Gail.

He liked the feel of her small hand in his.

The TV crew was waiting for them when they arrived at the Montauk Yacht Club, which had been named one of the top marinas in North America. It looked like the enclave of the rich and famous that it was.

Gail felt herself relax as soon as she saw Willow. Her friend was busy giving directions to the crew, and Russell stepped away to take a call, leaving her by herself.

She had tried to keep things all business between them, but every night her dreams were haunted by him. She had never been this turned on by a man. The week since they'd had their first date had been packed with things that kept her busy, but underlying that had been thoughts of Russell and a longing to be in his arms again.

Kat the production assistant came and got her. After she'd spent a little time in hair and makeup, Gail had her first inkling that this date wasn't going to be an entirely intimate one between her and Russell. Gail and Russell were positioned on the sundeck for the filming. The yacht was an Oceanfast 48 with four decks. There was a crew of ten and the yacht had a top speed of sixteen knots. Gail had no clue how fast that was, but since the captain had mentioned it, she thought it might be fast.

"Kat?" Gail asked as the PA finished adjusting her microphone.

"Yes?" she answered.

"Um…will you take a picture of Russell and me with my iPhone once he's ready?" Gail didn't feel silly asking. She knew she wanted something private of Russell that no one else would see. Something that wasn't a broadcast image or part of a promo package.

"Sure," Kat said with a smile. "You two make a nice-looking couple."

Russell arrived a few minutes later and was seated next to her, and for a minute Gail felt the family image in her head merge with reality.

"Do you mind if Kat takes a picture of us?" she asked Russell.

"Not at all," he said, putting his arm around her shoulder. They turned toward Kat and she snapped a photo of them with Gail's iPhone. She took her phone back and tried to slip away from Russell, but he kept her where she was, at his side.

"Why a photo?" he asked as Kat walked away. The sound people were doing a check, but no one was really paying much attention to the two of them.

"I just wanted to be able to remember this moment," she said.

Before Russell could respond, the production crew was moving around them and getting set up for their shots. They were given directions on how to sit and where to look.

"We're going to film you exchanging some small talk, and then we'll cut and remove all the microphones, and you can head out for your date. When you come back in, we will have you both record private video journals with your thoughts. Any questions?"

"Where's Jack?"

"In L.A. filming one of his other shows. We'll have you both chat with him via the magic of editing," Willow said.

Gail was beginning to feel as though the taped dates were routine. She was grateful that the producers—not just Willow—had agreed that the dates needed to have some privacy. It was hard to get to know someone when the cameras were rolling and they were both careful of what they were saying.

She wondered if this was what regular matchmaking would be like. Just staged dates and then feedback to the matchmaker? But she'd never know. This experience with Russell had convinced her that if he didn't work out, she was going back to her normal life.

"None here," Russell said.

Gail shifted away from Russell so she'd be in position as she'd been directed, but then she couldn't think of a thing to say once the cameras started rolling. Russell was watching her, and she nibbled on her lower lip.

Should she mention the media attention he'd been receiving, or how she'd signed a big A-lister as a new client? Should she talk about the times they'd seen each other since their last official date for the show? She really wished she'd taken a moment to ask a few questions of Willow, instead of just looking at Russell and lusting after him.

"It's a gorgeous day," she said at last.

"Yes, it is. Did you grow up near the water?" he asked.

"Not really," she said. "I'm from Texas…near Dallas. There were a few lakes near us."

"You don't have an accent," he said.

"Only when I'm home," she admitted with a laugh. "It didn't take me long to realize that if I was going to make a living talking to people I was going to need to be understood."

"Good point. When I first came here I realized that my accent was a novelty, but that I needed to know the idioms of American English if I was going to be successful."

"Exactly—we're speaking the same language, but sometimes we can't be understood," she said.

"A little bit like men and women," he said.

"True," she said, smiling at him. "Have you had that problem in the past?"

"Mostly I've learned to just sit back and let ladies talk. It's my experience that I don't get into as much trouble if I keep my mouth shut."

She had to laugh at him and the way he'd said that. She realized that she'd almost forgotten they were being taped. Russell had a way of commanding all her attention and making her forget everything else.

"You haven't been too quiet with me," she said.

"I'm trying a different tack with you," he said.

"Why?" she asked.

"You're too sassy. If I give you your way all the time, I'll lose myself," he said.

She shook her head, knowing he was teasing her. And she liked it. She liked seeing his big eyes twinkle as he tried to get a reaction out of her. "With that big head, you'd never get lost."

That startled a laugh out of him. And the director called, "Cut!" They were separated to have their microphones removed, and then the crew was gone, and it was just Russell and her and the yacht crew, who had been instructed to be discreet, according to Willow.

Gail went back to the bench seat as the boat ride got under way. She'd been out to the Hamptons for charity events in the summertime, but she'd always been working. This was the first time she could just relax.

Russell walked toward her holding two glasses, and she swallowed against a suddenly dry mouth. What she'd both wanted and dreaded for the past few days was about to happen. She was alone with Russell.

She'd told herself that he didn't need the distraction of getting involved with her while he was still dealing with Penny. But she couldn't resist her own desires any longer. No matter what happened today, she was going to go with it. She was going to stop worrying about the future and just enjoy this man who seemed to like her.

Normally Russell wouldn't even consider spending this much time away from the office when there was a deal in jeopardy, but it hadn't taken him long to decide that this afternoon he needed to leave his phone off. He knew that in the long run, winning over Gail was the more important project.

He handed her a glass of champagne and then sat down next to her. With the wind blowing through their hair, it was hard to have a deep conversation unless they sat close together.

"That was awkward," she said.

"How?" he asked. "I thought you were poised, as always."

"I had no idea what to say," she said. "I wasn't sure if I should mention the stuff that we've done away from the cameras."

"I think whatever we say will be fine."

"You think so? I've never been in a situation like this where I don't know what to do, you know? I'm used to being in charge and doing what I want."

Russell could honestly see that. It fit with her need for control. "We are still the decision makers, Gail. We can say no to anything they suggest."

"I know, but I figured I wasn't getting results being in charge…maybe it was time to let someone else decide things."

"I'll be happy to do that for you. Just put yourself in my hands," he said.

"I have a feeling we're talking about two different things," she said, biting her lower lip.

Russell didn't know if that was true. He could tell that Gail wanted him, and he was tired of playing games and pretending he didn't want her. The crew of the yacht were discreet, which was what Russell paid them to be. Now that they were underway the crew wouldn't bother them unless he summoned them. So in essence Gail and he were completely alone.

"I'll take care of you," he promised. But he wasn't sure that she could believe him. After everything that had happened, he knew he was battling, not just the fact that she didn't know him well enough to trust him, but also the fact that she'd seen some negative things about him.

"I don't need you to," she said.

"Yes, you do, you just don't trust me to," he said, gently.

Everyone wanted someone to watch over them. And he knew that Gail was no exception.

He stretched his arm out behind her on the seat and drew her into the curve of his body. She went there willingly, and he squeezed her to him. Her hair was stirred by the wind and brushed his neck and cheek. The strands were soft and smooth, and he lifted a hand to toy with one.

"I like this," he said.

"What?" she asked, tipping her head back to look at him.

"Holding you," he said. "I didn't know if you were ever going to let me again."

She reached up and weaved her fingers into his hand where it rested above her shoulder. "I didn't know if I would either. I really don't think this is wise."

"What?"

"Being with you. But I can't stop thinking about you. I hated being all business the last few days. "

He leaned down to kiss her, not wanting to let another opportunity to taste her go by. He'd realized a long time ago that life was too short to put off what he wanted for someday. His dad had done that but had ended up dying young. Never getting to the someday he'd been waiting for.

That was one of the reasons that Russell had never hesitated to do something when he felt the urge. And right now, his gut was crying out for more of Gail. He pulled her up and onto his lap.

She wrapped her arms around his shoulders and tunneled her fingers through his hair. He liked the feel of her on his lap. His erection stirred, and he ran his hands down her back to her waist, brought them together and then stroked his way up her front, cupping her breasts in both his hands. She moaned and shifted her shoulders so that her breasts moved in his hands.

He pulled his mouth from hers and looked down at her. Her skin was flushed with desire and her lips were once again swollen.

This time they were away from the office and the world. There was nothing to stop him from touching her.

She rubbed her hands down his chest. "I have had a lot of fantasies about what you look like with your shirt off."

"Have you?"

"Yes," she said. "You feel so muscled and I remembered the way your arms felt around me. I dreamed I was sleeping in them last night."

"I dreamed of these luscious breasts of yours pressed against me as I slid in and out of you."

She shivered in his arms. "I want you, Russell."

"Good."

She shook her head. "It's not good. I'm normally not this sexually aware of a man. It frightens me a little."

"It shouldn't. We are well suited to each other," he said.

She tilted her head a bit. "Does that mean you'd take your shirt off if I asked you to?"

"Yes."

"Consider yourself asked," she said.

He unbuttoned his shirt but didn't pull it off. She reached into the opening to touch him. Her fingers were cold against him but her touch was sure. She moved her hands up toward his neck and then pushed the sides of the shirt open so she could see his entire chest.

She leaned closer as she stroked her fingers down his sternum, lingering over the birthmark that was to the left of his nipple. Then she traced his nipple with her fingertip before leaning forward to kiss him.

He shuddered as her mouth met his chest and a shot of

pure energy went from through him. She shifted around on his lap until she was straddling him. Her fingernail traced the path further down his sternum to his belly button, and she circled it, making him harden even more. He was straining against his zipper. He breathed in deeply and all he could smell was Gail. He tunneled his fingers into her hair and tipped her head back, taking her mouth with his. He plunged his tongue deep into her mouth and, stroking deeply, moved it back and forth against her tongue. He couldn't kiss her deep enough to satisfy the ache her touch had stirred in him. He would never get enough of her, he thought.

But he was damned sure going to try.

Eight

Gail shifted on Russell's lap to let her fingers touch him more intimately. It had been almost a year since her last lover and, until Russell, she hadn't realized how much she missed the touch of a man. He smelled so good, and with the sun beating warmly on them, the sea breeze blowing around them and the relative isolation of being out on the water, she felt free. Free from the normal worries and doubts. Nothing could mar this.

Russell let her set the pace. She caressed his chest, which was warm and lightly covered in hair. She liked the way it tingled under her fingers as she ran them over the pads of his pectorals and down his ridged stomach. He had a tan, making her suspect he spent some time outside without his shirt on. The birthmark by his right nipple fascinated her with its shape, and she kept going back to touch him there.

"Unbutton your blouse," Russell said, his voice deep and husky with passion.

His commanding tone sent a pulse of liquid heat through her body. She shook her head. "I'm not sure I should."

"Do it. Now."

She nibbled on her lower lip and leaned in. "What are you going to do if I don't obey you?"

He arched one eyebrow at her. "Why wouldn't you obey me? It's what you want."

It was what she wanted. She leaned back on his thighs looking down at him and then scanning the horizon. There were no other boats in the area. She brought her hands to the first button and slowly undid it. She felt Russell's gaze on her as she moved to the next button. But she only pushed it through and then peeled the fabric back so he could get a glimpse of her lacy bra underneath.

"Are you teasing me?"

"Yes," she said. Russell made her feel more feminine, more alive than she had with any other man. He made her very glad that she was a woman and that she could excite him. She knew she was successful in turning him on because his erection nudged her under her hips.

She slowly undid the next button. "Is this what you wanted?"

"Almost," he said. "You are driving me out of my mind. I can't wait to see you naked."

"Do you like what you've seen so far?" she asked. She suspected he would because of the way he'd been with her up until this point, teasing her with kisses and his touch.

"Hell, yeah," he admitted. "But I'm desperate to see more of your body, beautiful," he said.

"Yes," she said, slowly unbuttoning the rest of her shirt. She held the blouse closed and leaned down to kiss him.

His mouth moved under hers with a smooth surety that made her know that Russell was still in charge of this. And she didn't care. She liked the feel of his tongue as it swept into her mouth. And she realized that even in just those short minutes they'd been apart, she'd missed the taste of him.

He slid his big, warm hands around her midriff and unfastened the back of her bra, before drawing her forward until her breasts brushed his naked chest. He pushed the fabric of her shirt off her shoulders and then leaned back to look at her. The sun was warm on her exposed skin, but the breeze was cool. She felt comfortable and safe on his lap with him watching her.

She wore a La Perla bra made of expensive lace that had a pretty, swirling pattern on the cups. He traced the edges of the demi-cups down to the V in the middle and back up the other side. "Beautiful."

She wanted to believe him when he called her that, but wasn't sure if he was merely referring to the exquisite lingerie she wore.

"You like pretty things on your body."

"I do," she said, even though it wasn't a question.

"If we go down to the stateroom will you take off your shorts and let me watch you?"

An image formed in her mind. "Will you keep your shirt off?"

"And probably take off a lot more," he said.

"Then, yes. I will do that."

"Good," he said, lifting her in his arms and carrying her across the deck. He walked down the few stairs to the galley, and then down a hallway to the master stateroom. Once inside, he set her on her feet and closed the door.

She stood there, feeling a little awkward now that he wasn't touching her. She wrapped her arms around her own waist, unsure what to do. But Russell banished her uncertainty with his touch, running his hand from her shoulder down her arm and taking her hand with his. He led her to the porthole windows where a chaise was situated. He leaned back on it.

"I'm ready."

"For?"

"I want to see if your panties match your bra. I want to see you, beautiful."

She nodded. She'd never undressed in front of a man before. Well, one time with one lover—they'd both stripped down quickly in front of each other, but she didn't think he'd even been looking at her. Certainly, he hadn't been staring at her the way Russell was.

"I've never done this before."

"You don't have to do it now, if you don't want to. But I want to see that pretty body of yours," Russell said. "I can undress you if that would be better."

She shook her head. She didn't want to miss this experience with him. She stood a few feet in front of him, where the sun shone through the porthole. She toed off her deck shoes, then put her hands at the waist of her shorts and unfastened them. She remembered how going slowly before had given her confidence and excited Russell, and she did it again.

After taking her time to lower the zipper, she pushed the shorts slowly down her legs. With a swivel of her hips, they fell to the floor. She stepped out of them and walked over to him. When she was close enough for him to touch, he reached out and stroked his hand down the outside of her thigh and then sprawled his fingers to clutch her.

"You are killing me," he said, drawing her closer between his legs. He wrapped his arms around her waist and kissed her belly button. She felt the warmth of his tongue and lips as he dropped kisses from her waist all the way down to her lower abdomen. He then used his tongue to trace the elastic band of her lacy thong along each of her hip bones.

She melted and her legs went weak. He lifted her up and pulled her onto his lap. She rubbed her center over the hard ridge of his erection, but it wasn't enough. She was empty and aching and needed more from him. She needed it now.

Russell was running his hands up and down her back. He found the fastener for her bra and undid it. Then very slowly he drew the straps down her arms and caressed his way from her back, up over her shoulders, and then down the front of her chest, until he was cupping both of her breasts in his hands. He palmed her nipples, abrading them lightly. She shivered in his arms.

He rubbed his thumbs in circles around both of her nipples as he leaned up to kiss her. His mouth was delicious. There was no other way to think of it. When he kissed her, she wanted to stay in his arms forever and let the sensations slowly sweep over her. He moved his hands to her back and drew her closer until the tips of her engorged nipples rubbed against the hair on his chest.

She shifted her shoulders and rubbed back and forth against him. She couldn't help moaning at how good it felt to have him touching her like this. She let her head fall back as she felt his mouth against the base of her neck. He dropped languid kisses against her exposed flesh. She felt the edge of his teeth as he scraped them against her neck and then suckled the base of it. Shivers spread throughout her body.

She reached between them, rubbing her hand up and down the ridge of his erection. She reached for the button of his pants but he stopped her.

"Not yet."

"Why not?" she asked, wanting more of him and wanting it now.

"Now I'm teasing you," he said.

He put his mouth back on her neck and slowly moved down her chest to the globes of her breasts, using his tongue to trace his way from the base of each breast to the tip of her nipple. But these were only teasing brushes of his tongue, nothing more. Finally she couldn't stand it another second and put her hands on his shoulders and shifted around until the tip of her nipple was pressed against his lips. He tongued her and she moaned his name. She wanted him. Now. She was tired of waiting and of denying herself.

He put his hands on her waist and held her to him as he suckled first one nipple and then the other. His fingers sprawled wide at her waist, and his hands roamed down to her buttocks to cup her backside. Using his grip on her waist, he shifted her back and forth over his erection. That hard ridge rubbed her in almost the right spot and she felt herself moistening, readying for him.

She reached between them again, unfastening his belt and then undoing his pants until she could reach her fingers inside and stroke him. She reached lower to brush her fingers over him.

He groaned her name. "Wrap your arms around me."

She did and he stood up. His loosened shorts fell to the floor, and he stepped out of them as she wrapped her legs around his lean waist. He walked them to the bed. She undid her legs and slipped down his body.

She pushed his boxer briefs down, carefully pulling the band over his erection. Then she pushed them down his legs and brought her hands back to him. She stroked him from tip to base and back again. He widened his stance to give her more access, and she continued to caress him as he did her.

He pulled her back to him and up over his lap. "I want you."

"Me too," she said.

"Good. I knew from the moment I saw you that I'd have you in my bed."

She hadn't been as sure.

He reached up and undid her hair until it fell around her shoulders. "Shake your head for me."

She did and felt him stir between his legs.

She shifted over him until the tip of his penis was at the entrance to her body. She started to move him, but he stopped her. "Are you on the pill?"

"Yes," she said. "And I know we are both healthy, since Matchmakers, Inc., ran a screening."

"I'm glad, because I don't want anything to come between us. I want to feel your warmth around me."

"I want that too. Enough playing around," she said.

"Yes," he said. He put his hands on her waist and positioned himself at the entrance of her body once more. He controlled her and entered her slowly, inch by inch, until he was fully seated inside of her. She threw her shoulders back and shuddered at the feel of him filling her. She tightened around him and he groaned deep in his throat.

"You feel so good," he said.

"Yes, you do too," she said.

He reached between their bodies and flicked his finger lightly against her clitoris. And she came. Just like that. With no warning, everything in her body convulsed in one second. She couldn't stop rocking her hips against him. Trying to take more of him. Then she leaned forward to find his mouth.

He broke away from the kiss and whispered hot words

in her ear. Once again, she felt the tingles spreading down her spine. "I'm going to come again."

"Not yet," he said. "Wait for me."

She didn't have to wait long, as she felt him tighten his grip on her waist, driving up into her. "Now."

She started spasming around him as he pulled her head to his and kissed her long and deep. She felt his release inside her body. He kept pumping into her and she shuddered around him, riding the crest of her orgasm until she collapsed against him.

She rested her head against his shoulder and he held her close to him as he rolled on to his side. She cuddled close to him as he swept his hand up and down her back.

"Thank you," he said.

"You're welcome," she said. She wrapped her arms around his shoulders and hugged him to her, finding the notch of his neck to rest her head for a few minutes, she wanted to rest in his arms. To let this moment turn into forever. She liked the feeling of him around her. He was warm, and she felt safe in his arms.

"I guess we should head back up to the deck," he said. "Do you want to wash up first?"

That broke the mood for her. She'd been feeling warm and happy with him, but now he was all business, and her heart broke a little. She didn't love him, but she'd thought…she'd thought this was more than a little afternoon sex. She saw now that it wasn't.

"I'll go first," she said, pushing herself up and moving to gather her clothes. "My blouse is upstairs. Will you get it?"

"Gail, are you okay?"

She nodded. She didn't want to talk about this. Not now. "I'm fine."

He cursed under his breath. "What did I say?"

"Nothing. Just get my blouse, okay?"

"I'm not going to let you brush this aside. We can't stay down here for too long. We're supposed to be back to the marina in thirty minutes."

"I know," she said. But she hadn't been thinking of the time or the show or anything except Russell. "Actually, I didn't. I lost track of everything except you."

But she doubted that he could say the same. He'd had one eye on the clock, and now they had to clean up and get back on deck before they returned to the marina. She hated this. She wished she'd thought more about the emotions that would be stirred up by going to a matchmaker and being on a reality TV show. It didn't matter that she'd thought she could control her reactions and be logical about this. The truth was she'd never be.

"I'm going to wash up."

"Gail—"

"Not now, Russell. I have to get back to normal, and then I can talk about this. Please get my blouse."

She walked to the head and closed the door behind her. It felt like a luxury bathroom—in fact, it was actually bigger than hers at home. It had a large garden tub and a shower big enough for two. She glanced at herself in the vanity mirror and saw her swollen lips and the redness on her neck from his kisses. She looked well loved. There was no way anyone would see her and not know that she and Russell had had sex.

She used a washcloth to wipe between her legs and then pulled her clothing on slowly, piece by piece. She put her hair back into the bun, and with each motion felt a bit more like herself. Except that she didn't have her blouse. She had to stand here in her expensive bra. She'd purchased it because she liked feeling sexy, but now she felt small and used.

It wasn't anyone's fault. She had expected…hell, she hadn't really thought about anything except making love to Russell. She'd wanted him and she'd had him, but she hadn't thought of the consequences.

There was a knock on the door. "Your blouse is on the bed. I'll meet you on deck."

"Thanks."

She waited a few more moments before opening the door and then quickly donned her blouse and buttoned it back up. The bed had been straightened and the room looked as it had when they'd entered it. No trace of them remained as she walked out the door and back up to the deck. Russell stood at the front of the yacht, looking out over the water.

She admitted to herself that her feelings for Russell scared her. Making love to him had only made her realize how vulnerable she really was. She wanted him to be that fantasy man she'd envisioned in her head, and that was a heavy burden for anyone, because fantasy was never going to equal reality. No matter how hard she tried to make it so.

He glanced over at her and smiled tentatively. She knew she'd thrown him too by the way she'd left the bed. But she couldn't help that. Russell was used to women and re-lationships that were fluid and changed on a dime, while she was used to…nothing, she thought. She'd never had a relationship with a man that had been real.

Russell was going to break her heart. She was honest enough to admit that to herself. She couldn't be around him and not fall a little for him, with his smoldering, sexy gaze and his easy charm. And he made her feel…beautiful. But now she realized she had to feel beautiful by herself, because depending on Russell was only going to lead her down a path she was afraid of.

Nine

As soon as they docked back at Montauk, the camera crews were waiting. Gail felt exposed and raw and wanted to get away from the prying eyes of the TV show she'd signed up for. Russell put his hand on the small of her back, and she looked up at him. Despite the fact that she wanted the distance from him at this moment, they presented a united front.

"I can't do this right now," she said.

"We have to or Willow will know…" he said.

"I…I'm going to say that I'm seasick. You can talk to them. Be charming and tell them what they want to hear. You are good at that."

"Yes, I am. I'm sorry."

"Don't be," she said. "The problem here is me."

"Gail—

"I can't."

"Yes, you can. You are trying to run away again. I'm not going to let you," he said.

"I'm not running."

"Yes, you are. We both signed up for this, and it's hard. I'm not denying that. I'd have loved to spend the rest of the afternoon in bed with you. If we'd been on my yacht, I would have told the captain to keep us at sea until we both decided we wanted to go back to the real world. But we don't have that choice on a date that was set up for us by a television show."

She nodded. "I get that. I just…I forget sometimes, and you never seem to."

He pulled her close and wrapped his arms around her. "One of us has to be aware of that stuff. I'd like nothing more than to just lose myself in you, but I don't want you to be embarrassed by anything that happens between us, and I want it to stay between us."

She pulled back and looked up at him. "I guess you haven't had a lot of privacy in your relationships."

"Try none," he said. "You are different to me, Gail, and I don't want to let anything screw this up."

"Okay. I'm sorry I overreacted," she said.

He shook his head. "You didn't. I was abrupt and should have handled that better. I have no excuses, except that you make me react like a primal man. All the charm and so-phistication I like to think I've accumulated over the years melts away when I'm with you."

She couldn't help but smile at that. She liked the thought of having that kind of power over him. It made her feel more equal because Russell made her vulnerable without really trying in the same way. She reacted to him as though he was the only man in the world made for her. And she knew that had to be because of all the emotions she'd built into the matchmaking thing. She didn't want to believe that it was Russell who was responsible.

"How was it?" Willow asked as she came onto the boat with the camera crew.

"Good," Gail said. Luckily, the sound tech was busy putting on the battery pack and wireless mic, otherwise she might have been forced to lie to Willow. A brief "good" was all she could manage. She hadn't intended on what had transpired between her and Russell. She shook her head and almost laughed out loud, but stopped herself.

"You okay?" Russell said, coming up behind her and putting his hand on her waist as he leaned in closely.

"No, but I'm faking it," she said and turned to him with a brilliant smile. "Is it working?"

He gave her a wry half smile. "Not when you smile like that. Right now it's not reaching your eyes as it usually does."

"I'm trying."

"And I appreciate that. I'm sorry, Gail. I shouldn't have—"

"No," she said. "Don't say any more right now. I can't deal with it and I might start crying."

Damn, she wasn't a crier. But her emotions were all tangled up, thanks to an afternoon of having sex with a man... whom she'd never expected to have sex with. A man who was charming and sophisticated and all the things she'd never expected to find. A man who was standing next to her, looking like he wanted to be her Prince Charming. And even though she'd learned a long time ago that she had to stand on her own, she wanted to lean on him. She wanted to feel those thick, comforting arms around her once again.

"You are going home with me after this," he said.

"I can't. I have a client meeting," she said. Her life went

on. This date was just one thing on her calendar today. And she'd deliberately scheduled something else so that she wouldn't be tempted by Russell. Damn, that had backfired. Big-time.

"We'll discuss this later," Russell said, as the director came over to them and gave them staging directions.

Gail was grateful for Russell, who took control of the postdate interview and did most of the talking, covering for her. She was trying to regain her equilibrium. Slowly she realized that what had panicked her was the fact that she'd felt as if she was like every other woman he'd slept with. But she knew that she was different. And Russell, for all his playing with the opposite sex, insisted that he saw her differently. By his own words, he wanted to be different for her, too.

She knew she was different with him. She'd never been that turned on by a man. Never come twice before, and never wanted to immediately crawl back into bed with any of her lovers. But Russell brought that out in her. She wanted him again.

"Gail?" he asked.

"Yes?"

"I asked if you'd like to go sailing again on my yacht. Maybe for a weekend where we didn't have to rush back for filming," he said.

"I'd like that very much," she said, speaking directly to Russell and looking into his eyes.

"Very good, I don't feel like we had enough time out there today," he said.

"Me either," she agreed. She wanted a lot more with Russell, and it didn't matter if every time she did something with him, she panicked. She was tired of hiding away from her own feelings, and she wasn't going to do it anymore.

* * *

Russell hadn't realized how gratifying it would be to step in and take care of Gail. He knew that she'd felt vulnerable when they'd returned to the Long Island Yacht Club and having him take control of the interview had helped her out. He'd never been a woman's hero and had never really wanted to be…until now. He wanted to do whatever he could to ensure that Gail would see her Mr. Right when she looked at him.

"That's a wrap. We'll see you both next week for your third date," the director said, and walked away.

"I have to talk to Willow and then I'm actually meeting my client at his home here in the Hamptons. So I won't be on the chopper with you on the way back," she said.

"I'll wait for you at the yacht club. Text me when you're ready," he said.

"Are you sure?"

"Definitely," he said. "I'm still hoping to talk you into going home with me."

"Fat chance," she said. "I need to process everything that happened."

"Process? Don't overthink it," he said. "Relationships aren't like business deals."

"I agree," she said. "But if I don't want to end up an aching mess, then I have to be sensible."

Within ten minutes they were both out of their microphones and free to go. Gail lingered, talking with Willow, as Russell waited to the side. His phone rang and he glanced at the screen, cursing under his breath as he realized it was Dylan.

"Holloway speaking," Russell said.

"Dylan here. I'm sorry to bother you, but I have Malcolm Addington of the Family Vacation Destinations group here in the lobby. He is asking if you can have dinner with him and his wife tonight."

"Give me a moment," Russell said. Malcolm had provided him with the excuse he needed to ask Gail out again. A date mixing business and pleasure was something that he suspected she wouldn't say no to. "Sorry to interrupt," he said, approaching her.

"It's okay," Gail said. "What's up?"

"A business dinner, and the other guy is bringing his wife…. Any chance you'd be available? I can accommodate your meeting," he said.

"I'll leave you two to work it out. Call me later," Willow said before she walked away.

Gail tipped her head to the side. "This feels like a setup, but I know you wouldn't lie about business."

"You're right. This dinner is kind of crucial. I'm trying to win this guy over to doing a merger. And I think you could help," Russell said.

"Okay, I'll do it. I can dine anytime after seven-thirty. I have to run to make my appointment. I'll meet you at the yacht club bar when I'm done."

"Thank you, Gail," he said.

She nodded, and he watched her walk away. Knowing her more intimately now, he couldn't help staring at her. He wanted her again. He hadn't been exaggerating at all when he'd told her that he wished they'd had more time together. He thought he'd covered his panic well by explaining his actions the way he had. But he knew deep inside that Gail had gotten too close. He wanted to be what she needed from him so that he could win her over, but he hadn't realized that he was creating a vulnerability in himself.

He, who never got attached to anyone, actually wanted

to keep Gail with him. Not just for today, but for the fore-seeable future. And that was damned scary.

His iPhone chirped at him, and he glanced down at the screen to see a text message from Dylan asking about dinner. He typed his response.

Tell Malcolm yes and make a reservation for four at the Rooftop Restaurant.

A moment later, he received a reply from Dylan.

Will do.

He walked up to the club and entered the air-conditioned bar area. He went to a corner table and ordered a Foster's. He was halfway through his second drink when he glanced up to see Conner walking toward him.

"How are the dates going?" Conner asked.

"Good—I think they are going very well," Russell said.

"Great. Um, my crew found something of yours on the boat," Conner said, and held out a lacy, delicate thong. The one that Gail had looked so lovely in.

"Thanks. I'd appreciate it if you didn't say anything more," Russell said.

"No problem," Conner said. "I didn't think about asking you to use your own yacht. The *Happily Ever After* is owned by Matchmakers Inc. We use it a lot for dates."

"That makes sense. Why are you telling me this?" Russell asked.

"Because I don't want to be ungentlemanly and say something I know I shouldn't," Conner said with that big grin of his.

"Good idea. Join me for a drink?" Russell invited.

"Love to," Conner said. "Let me go and order something. What are you drinking?"

"Foster's."

"Gone native?" Conner said with a laugh.

"I'm a Kiwi, not an Aussie," Russell said. But Conner was already walking away. Russell didn't dwell on it. Instead his mind drifted to Gail. He still couldn't figure her out. He wondered if he really needed to. He was kind of winging it with her and seemed to be doing okay, by his own estimation.

But he'd nearly lost her today. And that kind of mistake couldn't be made again. His problem was he didn't know many men who were in long-term committed relationships. And those he knew he wasn't going to ask for advice.

Conner returned and they talked about the America's Cup and the Americans' chances of winning this year. Conner knew the team captain and the conversation was enjoyable, but Russell couldn't concentrate on it. He was waiting. Every time the door opened, he refused to glance over and see if Gail had returned, but everything in him was anticipating the sound of her footsteps.

Finally she walked right up to their table. "Hello."

"Business done?" Russell asked.

"Yes."

"Do you know Conner MacAfee?" Russell gestured to his friend.

"Not personally. Nice to meet you," Gail said.

"The pleasure is all mine," Conner said, standing up. "I'll talk to you later."

Conner walked away, and Russell stood up. "Are you ready to go?"

"Definitely," Gail said.

He put his hand on the small of her back and directed her toward the entrance. And as they walked, he felt the eyes of other men on them and the answering primal need to stake his claim. To let everyone who saw them know that she belonged to him.

* * *

Gail had taken her time getting ready for her date with Russell. Things had changed and she wanted him to think it was no big deal. She was fairly sure that Russell didn't realize how out of character it was for her to sleep with a man on the second date. But she felt as though they'd known each other for much longer than they really had. There was something about Russell that made her feel more comfortable in her own skin than any man ever had.

She knew that was dangerous because she kept dismissing things that were red flags. Normally she would have stuck to her guns about not seeing him again tonight, but with Russell, she actually wanted to see more of him. She wanted to break plans with other people and do whatever he asked.

Damn, she was an idiot. She wasn't going to let him mean that much to her. She'd promised herself to be smart about this entire matchmaking thing. But one look into his light gray eyes had her swooning like a teenager in a Taylor Swift song.

She donned the new dress she'd purchased on her way home from work. Nothing ordinary or average tonight. She wanted Russell to be wowed, and she was pretty sure he would be. While she'd never feel truly pretty, she knew she looked good in the empire-waist sundress. Her shoulders were toned and her hair—which she left hanging around her shoulders in soft curls—looked perfect. Not a bit of frizz. Now, if she could just get the contacts in, she'd be ready to go.

The right one took her almost twenty minutes, and she lost the first one she tried to get in. She glared at her own face in the mirror. "Stop psyching yourself out."

But no amount of glaring made the stupid contact easier to get in. Finally it was in and she moved on to her left eye, which was always easier. Her mother swore that it was a mental thing, but Gail didn't care—she always got her left contact in with no effort. It was silly.

Finally she was ready and looked at herself in the full-length mirror in her bedroom. With her sandals on, she was taller, but that was not a problem because Russell was so tall. She looked almost as good as she did when the hair and makeup people helped her get ready for the TV show.

Suddenly unsure, she nibbled on her bottom lip. Was she fooling herself? Did the dress cling too much to her hips? Should she change?

She glanced at the clock and thought of grabbing her old standby black dress, but then shook her head. Feeling the weight of her own hair against the back of her neck, she remembered the way Russell had looked at her with her hair down in the mirror in his office. He found her attractive. Why would she doubt him?

She grabbed her clutch and left her bedroom before her doubts could influence her. She took the elevator down to the lobby of her apartment building and asked the doorman to get her a cab. A part of her knew that this was just fantasy. That what had happened between her and Russell that afternoon was making her see him through rose-colored glasses.

He was still a man with a lot of problems from his past tying him down. He was still someone she wasn't sure she wanted to trust. Yet her body wanted him, and her mind was slowly catching up.

The cab pulled to a stop in front of Daniel Boulard's restaurant on the Upper East Side. She'd never been here before but had of course heard of it. Who hadn't?

She calmed herself down, but when she walked into the lobby and saw Russell waiting for her in his dinner jacket and dress pants, her heart beat a little faster.

He looked good all the time, but dressed up, he looked great. He was meant to wear a dinner jacket, because it emphasized the width of his shoulders, and the white shirt accented his tan. He was yummy and dreamy, and when he looked up at her, she thought, he's mine.

He smiled at her, and she felt a tingle run through her body. She walked over to him and leaned up on tiptoe to kiss him. He hugged her close. "You look great."

"Thanks," she said, blushing. All the doubts she'd had and the frustration with the contacts melted away. She'd put herself through that to get this reaction, she thought. And it was all worth it.

"Malcolm and his wife are running a few minutes late. Would you like a drink while we wait?" he asked.

"I'm good for now," she said. "Tell me about Malcolm and what you need from me tonight."

"Just be yourself," he said. "He is a key player in a company I'd like to acquire, and he is one of those men who doesn't just let his pocketbook rule his business decisions. He wants to make sure I will keep the core of his company the same, and my values up to this point aren't what he has in mind."

"But you're changing," she said, wondering how much the matchmaking dates were being motivated by this business goal. She felt a little twinge of disappointment as she realized why Russell wanted her here, but he hadn't lied to her. She was the one who'd made it into something else in her head.

Those damned rose-colored glasses. She wished that this would be enough to make her see him as he really was, but she suspected it wasn't. Her heart was ruling her impressions of Russell now, and her mind had little to say, except to warn her that she was going to be hurt.

Ten

Malcolm and Ashley Addington were easily sixty years old, but looked at least ten years younger because they were fit and fashionable. Russell wondered why Malcolm would even consider selling the controlling shares in his corporation. But that wasn't his concern tonight. Convincing the father of four that Russell had changed from player to family man was his goal. And Gail was doing her part in making him seem like a changed man.

Russell normally would spend all evening trying to keep the subject on business, but having Gail at his side made a huge difference, and for the first time he realized why Malcolm was insisting on having a family man at the helm of his corporation. They talked about everything except business, and Russell was adept at keeping up with the conversation.

"How did you two meet?" Malcom's wife asked.

"Through a matchmaker. In fact, you will be able to see the details of our courtship this fall on a reality TV show."

"You're kidding," Ashley said. "I've never known anyone who was on those shows before. How did you even get on there?"

"The matchmaking service we'd both chosen is part of the show," Russell said.

Malcolm leaned across the table to look directly at Gail. "I can guess why he'd need a matchmaker, but why did you choose one?"

Gail blushed and looked at Russell. He reached over and took her hand under the table and squeezed it. She appeared to relax a bit.

"I wasn't meeting a lot of men who were good relationship material. Mostly I'm a workaholic, since I own my own company," she said at last. "But having a family is the next thing on my list. And I didn't want to waste any more time dating Mr. Wrong when a matchmaker could find me Mr. Right."

"Looks like you were successful," Ashley said. "You and Russell make a lovely couple."

"Thank you," Russell said. He didn't want to give Gail a chance to say anything about how he was less than perfect.

"You know, at first, Ashley, I wasn't sure Russell was a right fit for me," Gail said.

Russell wanted to groan or kick her under the table. Malcolm would love to hear her doubts about how he'd never be the right kind of man to settle down with. It would give the other man the excuse he needed to end the business discussions they'd been having.

"I can see that," Malcolm said. "Russell, you do have a certain reputation with the ladies."

"He certainly does," Gail agreed. "But once I got to

know the real man, well, it was easy to see that he was as ready for a change as I am."

"Really?" Malcolm asked.

"Yes," Gail said, looking over at him and smiling. "I think he's still got a way to go to be Mr. Right, but he's getting there."

Russell relaxed, truly relaxed for the first time that evening. He stopped worrying about Malcolm's impressions of himself, and Gail and took a deep breath as her confidence in him surrounded him. That was all he'd wanted from the beginning. Winning Gail over was hardly a done deal, but he was closer now than he'd been before, and he couldn't help the feeling of satisfaction that spread through him.

"It goes without saying that you are my Ms. Right," he said.

"Definitely," Gail said, then turned to Ashley. "Never let them see you sweat, right?"

"Oh, definitely. Malcolm still believes I wake up looking like this every day," Ashley said with a cheeky grin.

"And she still believes I have a six-pack," Malcolm said, rubbing the top of his belly. Which made both of them laugh.

Gail looked over at Russell, and he saw in her eyes that she wanted what the other couple had. That happiness that came from being so close to another person and being accepted for just who you are. He wanted that too, though even a week ago he'd have scoffed at the way Malcolm and Ashley were together. Since then, he'd changed.

"Shall we order dessert?" Russell asked.

"Definitely," Malcolm said. "And then I'll ask the ladies to give us some time alone to talk business."

"Well, you know my no-dessert rule," Ashley said. "I heard there is a nice view from the bar, so Gail and I can go get something yummy to drink there while you two discuss business."

"That sounds lovely," Gail said. "I want to know more about the decorator you mentioned earlier."

Russell stood when Gail did and dropped a kiss on her cheek. She hugged him and went up on tiptoe to whisper in his ear. "Knock 'em dead."

He squeezed her close. There were no words to express how grateful he was for what she'd done tonight. He doubted she even realized how much she'd helped him out, but he knew he owed Gail a lot.

"I intend to," he said.

She walked away, and he sat back down with Malcolm.

"You found a keeper."

"I did."

"I didn't believe you could change," Malcolm said. "I've been wary that you'd take our chain and turn it into another of your 'singles' vacation destinations. No matter what your assistant said, I've seen the way you operate."

"Well, I can understand that," Russell said, leaning back against his chair. "I'm in business to make money, and until this point in my life, I only knew one way to do it."

"But having Gail is making you see the world in a new light?"

Russell nodded. "The changes are kind of all happening together. I approached your corporation for a buyout at the same time I signed up for the matchmaking service."

"Why?" Malcolm asked. "You're not just using her to convince me you've changed, are you?"

Russell knew that Malcolm wasn't stupid, so he had to be careful how he answered that question. "I...I'm not going to lie. That was my initial thought, but once I met Gail, it was no longer about business."

Malcolm laughed a big, loud laugh that echoed around

the room. Several diners turned to look at them. "Caught in your own trap?"

"Definitely. And women aren't like business," Russell said.

"They certainly aren't. Lord knows Ashley has given me more trouble than any hotel I own," Malcolm said. "But she's worth it."

"I can see that. How long have you two been married?"

"Thirty-five years. She's the reason I'm stepping down. She wants to enjoy more time together and travel with me, instead of me working while she explores different places."

Russell wondered if he'd ever get to that point with Gail. Right now he was barely able to see them as a settled couple one year from now. But thirty-five years together? That was more than a lifetime.

"I think that's a great idea, and I am definitely the man to sell your shares to, so that you can enjoy your life and not worry about your business."

Being with Ashley made Gail keenly aware of how badly she needed this matchmaking with Russell to work out. Since they'd met, she'd been on a roller coaster of emotions, and tonight she'd seen how much he needed her to move his business deal forward. She shook her head as she thought about that. It worried her that he might be using her.

Again, she thought. She'd had a million different worries since she'd been matched with Russell, and this one was nothing new. He was so different from anyone else she'd met that it was hard to really understand what he wanted and how he acted.

"So…" Ashley said, as they had their Baileys-on-the-rocks, seated at the floor-to-ceiling window with a view of the city below them.

"So?"

"What's it like to date someone like Russell?" Ashley said. "Sorry if that's too forward, but Malcolm is so staid and always has been. I want to live vicariously through you."

Gail took a swallow of the Baileys and wondered exactly how to describe Russell. "I don't know what to say. It's sort of scary, because he has this reputation, and I'm just little old me. I worry that I'm not enough to keep him satisfied."

Ashley shook her head. "You're plenty. He was staring at you tonight when you weren't looking.... I've seen that before in men who are smitten."

Gail didn't doubt that. Even though Russell was selling it tonight, she knew he wasn't faking all of it. He did like her.

But his behavior gave her pause. She knew he wanted Malcolm and Ashley to see what they needed to see. And that was a couple in love.

"Russell is complicated."

Ashley nodded. "I can see that. Malcolm is too, but in a different way."

"How do you mean?" Gail asked. She was ready to hear about someone else and get the spotlight off her and Russell. She didn't want to have to lie to Ashley; she liked her.

"He's very strict about family time, and it's hard with all the kids. They have their ideas about what they want to do as adults, and our son Keir wanted to take over the company, but had other ideas about what direction it should go in...." Ashley shook her head. "Sorry."

"It's okay. Right now, since we are in the beginning of our relationship, I just assumed that once we were as settled as you and Malcolm, things would just be good all the time."

Ashley laughed. "They are good. Better than good. But it's hard once you have kids, because they add a new dimension to every decision you make. You'll see someday. Malcolm compromises a lot, because family is at the core of everything he does."

"Did you know that when you married him?"

"Yes. I wanted to be a stay-at-home mom and have him take care of me and our children, and he always has."

"Sounds perfect," Gail said. She knew that wasn't the relationship either she or Russell desired. Though she wanted kids, she knew that she still needed her career. It was too much a part of who she was for her to give it up.

"Do you really want to know more about my decorator?" Ashley asked.

"Not really, but it seemed the right thing to say."

Ashley laughed. "I've had to do so many of these wife chats, I understand. I did want to ask you a little more about what you do."

"Ask away," Gail said. "I own my own public relations firm and give my clients advice on what to say and when to say it."

"Does it work? I've often wondered how celebs get into trouble if they have people like you working for them," Ashley said.

"It only works if the client listens to you. My company is usually hired after the client has said or done something out of character for them. So, like a sports figure who gets caught in a compromising situation, or an actor who badmouths a director. Stuff like that."

"What do you to fix that?" Ashley asked.

"We can't fix it, exactly, but we do damage control. Show them in the light they used to be in, maybe get them a guest spot on *Dr. Drew*. Something to show that they know they screwed up. Let's face it, we're all human and we all make mistakes."

"Very true. And I like to see celebs like that," Ashley said. "Makes them seem more real."

"Yes, it does," Gail said, knowing that Russell was like the celebs she dealt with. If she'd been his PR person, she would have definitely recommended he find a woman like herself and do some sort of public courtship to "fix" his image.

Gail didn't want to think that Russell was using her, but tonight she really had no choice. She wondered if she'd have the guts to confront him on it.

Russell helped Gail into his waiting car and then slid in next to her. She'd been quiet since they'd joined back up together, and he wondered what she was thinking.

"Thank you."

"For what? Dinner was nice, but I doubt you are thanking me for that," she said. She seemed pensive and very closed off to him. It wasn't what he'd expected, since the evening had gone beyond his expectations and, if he was honest, he wanted her to be happy and celebrate with him.

"For tonight. You were spot-on and exactly what I needed in a partner."

"I kind of picked up on that," she said.

He stretched his arm along the back of the seat and toyed with a strand of her hair as the driver maneuvered them through the crowded city streets. "I appreciate everything you did. Malcolm is a nice guy, but he has some odd ideas about his business and won't sell—"

"I know. I got that from the first moment we met him. And Ashley confirmed it when we were alone. Did you know he won't even let his son take over?"

"I didn't know that," Russell said. "Why not?"

"Something about not following his vision," Gail said. "Are you playing a game with me, Russell?"

"No. I am ready for a change. As I've said a million times to you. When are you going to believe me?"

She shook her head. "When you stop surprising me. First it was your starlet ex-girlfriend, now it's a man who will only sell his company to a settled man. Every time I think I have you figured out, it's something else."

Russell really didn't have an answer to that. "You're just as a complex. Maybe even more so, because all of my issues are out in the open, and you play yours close to the chest. Slowly letting me see a bit of you and then pushing me away again."

Gail nibbled on her lower lip and turned in the seat so she was facing him head-on. "I'm not trying to tease you."

"I know that. Starting a relationship is hard for anyone. We both are complex people, and we have to do it on camera and in the middle of things that keep coming up. It's hard."

"It is hard. And you're right, I do play things close to my chest. It's just that every time I decide it's safe to trust you, something else comes up that makes me leery again."

Russell wished he had the words to assure her that everything would be okay, but he didn't know that, and he wasn't about to lie to her. "I wasn't acting tonight. I think we make a really good couple."

"I think we do too. But I'm not sure that means we should be a couple. You know, there are women out there who act as corporate wives," Gail said.

"There isn't another woman I want by my side, Gail. You are the one who understands me, and we fit together."

She blushed. "We do fit together."

He smiled at her. "Not just physically but also socially.

We were good together tonight. There aren't a lot of couples who are that in sync with each other."

He'd seen that enough in his friends and even with the other women he'd dated. No one fit him as completely as Gail did. And that was something he wasn't going to let slip away.

"We are in sync. I'm kind of surprised, given the lifestyles we both have led."

Russell was too. "Maybe that's why we were matched to each other."

"You have a point. From the beginning, I've been trying to figure out exactly why we were matched up."

Russell smiled at her. "Sounds like you. What have you come up with?"

She shrugged her shoulder and looked back out at the street. "Nothing, Russell. Until tonight I couldn't see whatever the matchmaker saw in us. Until we were at that table chatting with another couple—a real married couple—I didn't have a clue of why we were together."

"And after dinner, you figured it out?" he asked. He didn't care why they were together, but he knew it was important to Gail. He just wanted them to stay together and to be happy. He liked her, he needed her. And as far as he was concerned, he'd hit the lottery when he'd been paired up with Gail. She was everything he wanted in a woman and potential wife, and so much more.

"I think I did," she said.

"Tell me what you figured out," he said.

"I figured out that we are the same on some level. We both know how to socialize, and we have similar tastes."

"And that was enough for the matchmaker?"

"No, we also each have something the other one needs—I have the reputation and stability that you needed, and you have that romantic hero quality that I've long wanted."

Russell didn't like the way that sounded, and had the feeling that Gail didn't see those things in a positive light either.

"We have what's missing in each other," he said. "We complete each other, Gail, and I don't know why you can't see it."

"How do you mean?"

"You're cautious where I'm adventurous. I'm wild where you are calm. And that's what makes us fit together. You want to be adventurous, but have always been afraid, and you've always wanted to be a little bit wild, but were scared you might lose yourself. But, now that you have me in your life, you can be those things and know that I will keep you safe."

Eleven

Gail chose a relatively tame outing for their next filmed date. It was a pizza-making class that she'd been wanting to try but only couples could book.

"Pizza, eh? I don't know that I've ever made one," Russell said, as they entered the kitchen area with a view of the Hudson River at their back.

"Do you cook?" she asked.

"I'm single—what do you think?" he countered.

"I bet you can make one or two things and that's it," she said. She figured a bachelor like Russell wouldn't have to cook for himself too often.

"You'd be right. If I can toss it on the grill or in the microwave, then I call it a meal."

"That sounds a bit limited," she said.

"After tonight, I'll be able to make pizza with the best of them," he said.

"Okay, people, let's get the lights set up and you two

into makeup," Willow said, as she entered the room. "Kat, I need you to confirm that everyone in the class tonight has signed the waiver to allow them to be filmed."

"I'm on it, boss," Kat said.

Willow went off to tell more people what to do, something that Gail realized her friend did really well. And she and Russell were sent to their respective hair and makeup people. She was almost getting used to how she looked when she was done up for the show. But she'd asked them to stop straightening her hair, which they had agreed to do.

Soon she was wired with her microphone and directed to a cooking station. Other couples were trickling in and, as she waited for Russell, Gail smiled at some of the men and women who were glancing over at her, making her feel a little self-conscious. Finally Russell walked up beside her, and Gail breathed a sigh of relief—until she heard some of the people talking among themselves about Russell.

"Oh, ho, this is going to be a fun night," she said. "I guess I should have chosen something where we'd be alone."

Russell put his arm around her and squeezed her close. She tried to ignore the fact that he soothed some of her nerves with that simple little touch.

"Nah, this is going to be perfect," he said.

"What makes you say that?"

"The fact that you picked it," he said with that sexy grin of his.

"May I have everyone's attention, please," Willow said, moving to stand in the center of the room. "Chef David will be out in a moment, and your class will begin. I need you all to just act natural and try to ignore our cameras.

We are going to tape the session uninterrupted and then edit it, so that we don't interrupt the class."

"What are you filming?" a man on the other side of the room asked. "Will we be on TV?"

"We are filming a reality dating show, and you might be on TV, but we won't be filming you up close," Willow answered. "Any other questions?"

Willow moved over to Gail and Russell's station. "For you two, just do what you've been doing. We are going to have a camera on you both, and we will be recording your conversations. The focus of this episode isn't learning to make pizza, but rather on your date, okay?"

"Yes," Gail said.

"Of course," Russell answered.

Willow moved away, and the chef came in and started the class with a brief lesson in the history of pizza. Then he talked about where he came from in Italy and how they made it there. The chef was from Naples.

"Have you ever been to Italy?" Russell asked.

"No. I'm hoping to go on a Mediterranean cruise next summer, but I'm usually busy and so are my friends, so…"

"You work too hard," Russell said.

"Ha. That's a laugh coming from a workaholic like you. Have you been to Italy?"

"Yes, Rome and Venice," he said.

"Do you have Kiwi Klubs there?" she asked.

That surprised a laugh out of him, and he shrugged. "In fact, I do. But I did take some time off to sightsee while I was there."

She was going to ask him more about it, but the chef was having them take a bowl with prepared dough in it out from under their table.

"I will now show you how to toss the dough," Chef David said.

He tossed it in the air, expertly expanding it with each successive toss, working the dough until it was the right size for the pizza mat on the table.

"Now you try it," Chef David said.

"Right," Gail said under her breath. "Why don't you go first?"

Russell picked the dough up, and after a moment of stretching it, he started tossing it. With each toss it remained the same size. She watched as he got more frustrated at the dough. "Damn, it's harder than it looks."

"Is it?" she asked.

"You have a try," he said.

He handed her the dough, and she started to toss it in the air. It was hard to get it to stretch, so after three unsuccessful tosses, she put the dough back in the bowl.

"Let's try pulling on it," Russell said.

They each got a side of the dough and stretched it until a big hole opened in the center, and Gail started laughing. Russell looked up at her and laughed too. What had struck her as funny was that they were both so successful and used to making things happen, this stupid pizza dough should have been a snap, but it wasn't.

Russell was concentrating on it as though he could will the dough into the right shape. Chef David heard them laughing and came over to offer some additional guidance.

But even he had to shake his head at the pathetic way their dough looked. They formed it as close to a pizza shape as they could on the tray.

"Thank you," Russell said after the chef walked away and they were alone.

"For?"

"Tonight. It's fun and silly and just the release I need from all the pressure that has been hounding me."

She smiled at him. "I'm glad."

But, inside, she wasn't too sure about that. She was still scared of caring too much about Russell. Tonight he was that guy she needed him to be, but she'd heard the comments of the other participants. Everyone knew that Russell was the love-'em-and-leave-'em bachelor type, and Gail wanted to believe she wasn't heading for a heartache, but wasn't too sure.

When the class was over and they were all allowed to take their pizzas to the patio outside the cooking school, Gail was surprised to see paparazzi waiting for them. Russell's face got tight and they both tried to ignore it, but reality was setting back in. Russell wasn't the carefree guy she needed him to be. He had real problems, and the only reality between them was the matchmaking show. They wrapped up the evening with a quick chat with the host. But Gail slipped away while Russell was still talking to Jack. She needed to escape and figure out if her feelings were real of just another part of this show.

Russell knew that last taped date hadn't ended as well as he'd hoped. He had thought long and hard about what he wanted to do on his next date with Gail, but the constant barrage of media attention and the problems with Penny kept him from being able to select the date he wanted. So he settled for walking the Appalachian Trail near Sunrise Mountain in New Jersey.

"I don't know about this," Gail said, as they were fitted with microphones before the hike.

"I'll protect you," Russell said.

"I'm sure you will try," she said. "But what about bugs and stuff?"

He laughed nervously. He was very afraid that, when the television show ended, Gail was going to walk out of his life without a backward glance. "You'll be fine."

She looked like a city girl in her walking shorts and newly purchased hiking boots. She had her thick hair braided down her back and a pair of cute designer sunglasses perched on the end of her nose. He wanted her.

He wanted to take her out into the woods and find a secluded place to make love to her, but with the cameras rolling that was impossible. Far away from the pressures of both of their jobs and lives. He needed to be buried in that long, silky body of hers, so he could hold her and pretend that she was his.

"So, for filming," Willow said, "I'm thinking we will do a shot of you guys here at the start of the trail and then one at the summit. I'm sending two of our crew up the mountain ahead of you so they can do some long shots. I want the date to be yours, but I need some good footage too."

"That's fine," Russell said. "Do they need a map? Or do they know where they're going?"

He had spent a month hiking the trail last year before he'd started dating Penny. He'd needed to get his head together, and hiking had helped. Once he'd grown in his beard and spent a few weeks out here, no one had recognized him and he was just another man, another hiker.

"It'll be okay," he said to Gail.

"It's just not my thing," she said by way of explanation.

"Pizza making wasn't mine but it turned out okay," he said.

"Until the end of the night," she reminded him.

"That's the beauty of this place. No paparazzi out here. Too much work for them," he said.

She laughed, as he'd hoped she would. "Okay, tell me what to do.... You've done this before, right?"

"Yes, I have. I know what I'm about in the outdoors," he said.

"That's right. You grew up on a farm, didn't you?" she asked.

"A ranch," he corrected her.

"Okay," Willow said, interrupting them. "Go ahead and start hiking."

As they got underway, Russell wanted to be alone with Gail, instead of having the cameras there. He hadn't had a chance to talk to Gail in days. But he wasn't going to have privacy right now.

"How have you been?" she asked.

"Fine."

"Really?"

"No," he said. "The media are making some demands on me, and I still have a lot of work to do. There hasn't been any time to chat with you."

She reached out and snagged his hand, twining their fingers together. "You can always call me."

He squeezed her fingers and lifted their joined hands to his mouth, brushing his lips across the back of her knuckles. "I've missed you."

"Why?" she asked.

"You just treat me like a regular guy. And there's no chaos when you're around," he said.

She blushed. "That's sweet."

Now he felt like an idiot. He didn't want to be sweet. He wanted to be…whatever she really needed from him, and he knew on an instinctive level that he wasn't. It didn't stop him from trying but, he knew he was missing the boat.

"I'm sorry."

"For what?"

He thought about it for a minute. Finding the words to tell her that he knew he wasn't the man she wanted was harder than he'd thought it would be. "For not—ah, hell, I don't know. I just wish that my life was more normal for you."

She chewed her lower lip as they continued walking, and then she stopped. "I know that I haven't been very easygoing about everything that is happening in your life right now, but that doesn't mean I regret meeting you or these dates."

"Good. I don't either," he said.

He led them up the trail, and when they reached the peak, he pulled her into his arms and kissed her. The camera crew was waiting and caught the entire thing on tape, but Russell didn't care. He had found something with Gail that he'd never expected, and he wasn't about to change his attitude and let her slip away.

She was his. And it was time for Gail and everyone else to know that.

Gail spent the next week trying to just relax and let her fears dissipate, but it was hard. She knew that Russell wasn't the type of man to ever need a matchmaker. The last two dates they'd had were fun, and she'd fallen just a little bit more for him on each occasion, but it was the time away from the camera that was making her wonder if he was sincere and that worried her. Was she seeing the real man or the man he wanted her to see?

"Why are you frowning?" Nichole asked as she took a seat next to Gail and Willow at the Blue Fish. It was rare that the three friends got a chance to catch up.

"Was I?"

"You know you were. Don't make me ferret the truth out of you. I'm a reporter—that's what I do for a living."

"I know. I'm not sure—

"Don't say another word," Willow said. "I need a drink

and I don't want to miss any of the gossip." She got up and went to the bar.

"You won't," Nichole reassured her. "Don't think you're getting out of telling us what's going on, Gail."

"I know I'm not. So much has happened since last month."

"For me too," Nichole said. "I've been researching Matchmakers Inc., and I talked my boss into letting me do a story on Conner MacAfee. Have you met him?"

"Yes. He and Russell are friends," Gail said.

"What did I miss?" Willow said, as she returned to the table with a round of drinks.

"You didn't miss anything," Gail said with a laugh. "Nichole is doing a story on Conner MacAfee."

Willow sat down on the seat next to Gail and plopped her wineglass on the table. "I'm exhausted."

"You always are," Gail said.

"Running a production is stressful. You and Russell have been great."

"Thanks. We try to do our best," Gail said.

"Okay, so back to whatever I interrupted," Willow said.

Gail took a long swallow of her Pinot Grigio, letting the dry wine soothe her nerves. "I don't know what we were talking about."

"Liar," Nichole said. "She was frowning. Something is bothering her."

Gail shook her head. "I'm…I don't want to talk about it."

"It has to be Russell. Tell us about him," Nichole said.

"I wonder if I should tape this for the show," Willow said.

Gail kicked her under the table. "Can I please have one thing in my life that is private?"

"It was just an idea," Willow said. "He's a very public man."

Gail leaned back in her seat. "That's part of the problem. How much of dating me is for real, and how much of it is for show?"

Willow put both elbows on the table and leveled her ebony gaze on Gail. "He signed up with Matchmakers Inc., the same as you did. And we didn't ask for him, he was the man the matchmaker picked for you."

"Why?" Gail asked. She knew that Russell had explained it, but it was hard for her to believe that a man as dynamic as he was would be the perfect match for her. How could that be? They weren't the same—they were like oil and water, and that didn't seem like a peaceful way to live.

"I don't know," Willow said. "But I do know that when I watch you two together, something just clicks. Whatever your fears are, are you sure they are based on Russell? And not your own doubts in men?"

Gail couldn't answer that. She knew she had issues. She'd been battling them all along and trying to be as open and trusting of Russell as she could be. Was she making a big deal out of nothing?

"That's why I'm frowning, Nic. I can't figure this out. No matter which way I look at this, I'm still unsure."

Nichole reached over and patted her hand. "I don't blame you. That's why I've stopped dating."

"Yeah, right," Willow said. "I saw you in the club the other night with a guy."

"That's sex, ladies. Not dating," Nichole said with a laugh.

Gail shook her head. Nichole was wild and had a joie de vivre that she'd never had. "You'd be better suited to Russell."

"No, I wouldn't. We'd bore each other in no time. Sex is a temporary bond. But you are building, or want to build, a relationship. That takes something different."

"It takes trust," Gail said. And that was where she struggled. If she could simply trust Russell and ignore her doubts there would be no problem. "Enough about me. Tell me what's going on with you two."

"Willow let slip that I'm hooking up with a hottie, so I guess I have nothing new to say."

"Who's the hottie?" Gail asked.

"A young photographer at the paper. He is Spanish and likes older women as lovers.... He said that to me. I was like, hey, I'm only thirty. Then I realized, girls, we're thirty!"

Gail laughed at the way Nichole said it. "I already knew that."

"Me too," Willow said. "But then Gail and I aren't out there dating like we're still twenty-five."

"Hey, one of us has to enjoy life while you two are busy putting your nose to the grindstone. You can live vicariously through me."

Gail laughed as she knew Nichole intended them to, but a part of her was worried about her friend. Where Gail wore her lack of trust on her sleeve, Nichole hid hers deep behind a wall of superficial dating and a lifestyle that seemed wild and carefree. But Nichole had her secrets, just the same as Gail did.

"How many more dates do you have?" Nichole asked.

"Two. We are nearing the end, and I for one will be glad."

"Will you keep seeing him?" Willow asked.

"Yes," Gail said. "I think I will. He's been so busy with a business deal and that bad press from Penny, that we are hoping to enjoy some quiet time once filming stops."

"That's good," Willow said. "We want to see some big romance at the end. The other producers are urging him to ask you to marry him."

Gail swallowed hard. She wasn't sure she wanted that to happen on camera. "That doesn't seem right."

"I know. Russell said he'd ask you when he was good and ready."

Gail felt a little better, and the fear that had been riding her abated a little. Maybe she and Russell really were meant to be together.

Twelve

Poker night with the boys was always one of Russell's favorite occasions, but he had a date with Gail and, for once, he was anxious for the game to end. He shouldn't have been surprised; he wanted to spend every minute he could with Gail—she was all he thought about. And thanks to the producers of *Sexy and Single*, now all he could think about was asking her to marry him.

He didn't know if six dates were enough to ask her to spend the rest of her life with him. He wasn't entirely sure he wanted to commit himself to Gail now because of how busy he was, and he knew that, if he asked her to marry him, she would expect him to be a good husband.

Tonight he was playing at Conner's penthouse apartment with Conner, Gerald McIntyre and Les Wells. Gerald and Les were friends of Conner's. They went outside to smoke cigars after an hour of playing, and Russell contemplated leaving the game. He'd broken even, but that wasn't how he normally played. He liked to win at poker, as he did at everything, but he was distracted by Gail.

He still wasn't sure he'd figured out what she needed from Mr. Right. Plus, how was he going to juggle that on top of the new merger, which appeared to be going through? At least he had a little thank-you gift for Gail for her part in making that happen.

"Just because you look at your watch doesn't mean time will go faster," Conner said.

"Am I that obvious?" Russell asked.

"Yes. What are you rushing off to?" Conner asked.

"A woman."

"Gail?"

"Yes."

"Good. I take it you're pleased with your match?" Conner asked, taking a sip of his rye whiskey.

"Very pleased. I wouldn't have thought an interview and a questionnaire would do the job.... Well, who does think that matchmaking works?"

Conner laughed. "You'd be surprised at how much more is involved than that."

"Have you had a hand in any of the matches?" Russell asked.

"Not at all. My assistant tells me I'm not intuitive enough," Conner said with a laugh. "My grandmother said the same thing. She's the one I inherited the business from."

"Did you believe her?"

"Hell, yes. I barely know what I want, much less have the ability to guess what a woman wants," Conner said, shaking his head. "I have no idea how you are managing Gail so successfully. Why did you want to give up the single lifestyle?"

Russell wasn't too sure how honest to be, but this was

Conner, and he'd been in the same situation as Russell before. "I was getting bored with it. After so many years of serial dating, every woman was becoming the same. I wanted...something different."

Conner nodded. "I hear ya. Sometimes I think I should give it a whirl."

"You should," Russell said.

Conner arched one eyebrow at him. "My mother says the same thing. She's anxious for grandbabies. Do you have kids?"

"No."

"What about those paternity suits?"

"Just lump-sum settlements to help the mothers. I'm not the father."

"Why would you do that?"

"The women were friends.... They needed some help and I was in a position to help them."

"Really? Why would you do that?" Conner asked.

"To be honest, it was to help my business. I was just starting out when the first suit came up. Had just made my first million and the lawsuit brought people to the Kiwi Klub like you wouldn't believe. The kids weren't mine," Russell said, thinking that at some point he was going to have to tell Gail that he was sterile. But right now, he had bigger problems.

Conner looked at the glass door leading to the balcony as if to make sure they were still alone. "Why not just do that with Penny?"

"She is insisting the baby is mine. And it's not. As soon as she's honest with me, I'll help her out."

"Does she know that?" Conner asked.

"I've told her as much," Russell said.

"What does Gail think about that?" Conner asked. "I

can't imagine she's too happy with the thought of you giving money to Penny."

Russell and Gail didn't talk too much about Penny. They had dealt with the paparazzi when they had to. And Gail had offered him her professional opinion on the matter, but he'd been frank with Gail and let her know where he stood. "I think she's fine with it. We've discussed Penny and my past suits."

Conner shook his head. "You're a better man than me."

"Doubtful," Russell said.

"I would never settle a paternity suit," Conner said. "My mother would be livid. She'd want to raise the kid as a MacAfee."

"That's the difference between you and me. You were born with a silver spoon in your mouth and have the generations of family waiting for you to give them an heir. I am the orphaned son of a down-on-his-luck rancher.... No one questions me."

Conner nodded. "I envy you. Someday I'd like to just walk away from my family and my name. But I think it would kill my mother."

"She's in ill health?"

"No, but my sister and I are all she has left. And she relies on me far more than you'd imagine."

Russell wondered what that would be like. He sort of envied Conner and that legacy he had. His family had the big mansion in the Hamptons, and he had a family history he was proud of. Russell imagined that was what he'd have with Gail. But he knew there'd be no child to pass that on to, and that worried him a bit, because, as he'd come to know Gail and in talking to her about Penny's situation, he'd realized that she wanted a large family one day.

And while he could give her anything else in the world

she desired, a family of her own was beyond his reach. "I'm glad you have each other."

Conner nodded, but the other men rejoined them and the game play resumed. Russell wasn't as anxious to get to Gail as he had been before. He was afraid for the first time that he might not be holding a winning hand with her after all.

Gail left her friends and headed uptown toward home. Russell had asked if he could come over tonight, and she'd said yes. She'd been pretty successful in not sleeping with him again. Not because she hadn't wanted to, but because she'd been afraid that if she did, she'd have to admit she was falling in love with him.

She let the night doorman know that Russell would be coming by and to let him up. His last text had said he'd be leaving ten minutes ago, so she felt she might be just ahead of him.

They'd been busy between their on-air dates, and there simply hadn't been a lot of time to get together. When he'd texted earlier tonight, asking if he could stop by, she hadn't wanted to deny herself the chance to see him and be with him again.

Despite what she'd said to Willow and Nichole, she really had no idea if she and Russell would see each other after the show ended. She suspected they'd both say they wanted to continue dating, but they were very busy people and, for her part, Gail knew she was still afraid to let Russell in. Still afraid to really trust him, and being in love... falling in love, wasn't going to help that in the least.

She let herself into her apartment and turned on the lights in the living room. She kicked off her shoes in her bedroom and then slowly walked through her empty place. Her dreams had been changing over the last four weeks as she'd come to know Russell. Now, instead of that face-less man she'd fantasized about for years, she saw Russell standing next to her. She saw him as the husband and father in her little perfect-family image.

The doorbell rang, and she felt her heartbeat speed up as she went to let Russell in. His hair was rumpled and he smelled faintly of cigars. But he smiled when he saw her and stepped over the threshold to take her into his arms.

He kissed her long and hard, and the doubts she'd had subsided. She'd missed this, she thought, closing her eyes and resting her cheek on his shoulder. When they were apart, it was easy to entertain her doubts, but when she was in his arms, she felt like she'd found that thing she'd always been searching for. She was afraid to admit to her-self that being in his arms felt like home.

"That's more like it. I can't believe it's been two weeks since I've held you like this," he said.

"Me either. Do you want a drink?" she asked, leading the way to the living room.

"No, I'd like to hold you in my arms," he said. "I've missed that, beautiful."

"I've missed you," she said. "But I see you've been busy. Every alert I get for work has at least one mention of you or Penny in it."

"Yes. She is going ahead with her plan to blame her pregnancy on me."

"Has she had—

"I don't really want to talk about her," Russell said. "Sorry to interrupt you, but I have some good news."

She smiled at him, even though she suspected he wasn't sorry at all. He didn't like talking about Penny or the neg-ative media she'd generated for him. "What's your good news?"

"Malcolm has accepted my offer to buy his shares. In

a short while—maybe two months—I will be the controlling owner of Family Vacation Destinations."

"That name stinks. You're going to have to change it," Gail said. "But congrats. I know that is what you wanted."

"Yes, the name will be changed," Russell said, reaching into his pocket. "I wouldn't have convinced Malcolm without your help, and I want to say thank-you."

He held a small blue jewelry box out toward her, and she hesitated. "Your thanks are enough, Russell. I don't need a gift."

"Please accept this. I want you to know that helping me out with Malcolm and Ashley was a big part of closing this deal. And it had nothing to do with our courtship."

Courtship. It was an old-fashioned word, but it made sense in thinking of the arranged dates they'd been on. "In that case, I'll be happy to accept it."

She took the light blue Tiffany box from him and opened it to find another velvet box inside. She tipped it out into her hand and then opened the hinged lid. Lying there were a pair of earrings. Chocolate pearls encircled by diamonds. They were beautiful. She hadn't received a gift like this from a man in a long time.

"Thank you, Russell."

"You're welcome," he said. "Put them on."

She did and then swept her hair up so he could see them. "Gorgeous, but then, I knew they would be. I know that our dates with the matchmaker are ending…. Well, we have two more, but I don't want to stop seeing you."

"Good," she said. "I know we're both busy."

"Not too busy for each other. I know you had your reasons for going to the matchmaker, and I don't think they've changed."

"They haven't."

"Do you think I can be your Mr. Right?" he asked.

Gail didn't know. She wanted to say yes, but there was still a part of her that wasn't sure.

"I guess not," Russell said.

She shook her head. "You are Mr. Right in my eyes now, but I'm scared, Russell, because I don't know if I'm trusting you because of your charming ways, or if you are the real deal. And I don't want to get hurt."

"How is this different from how you felt when you first saw me?" he asked. "Haven't you seen that I'm not the same man who was a serial dater?"

"Yes, I have. And the way it's different is that I really care for you now, and I don't want to risk being disappointed by you."

"Then let me take care of you. I'm not going to let you down, Gail."

She shook her head, but he kissed her and then made love to her on the couch, and all her objections disappeared. All she could think about as he held her close was that she wanted to always be in his arms. No matter what the consequences were.

Thirteen

Gail hadn't had a man sleep over in a long time. And Russell wasn't just any guy. The way she felt about him was more intense and, honestly, she wasn't sure how to act this morning. She had the usual fears—morning dragon breath, hair that was more than tousled, thanks to its being curly and tending to stick out all over the place, and of course no makeup. She didn't have great skin like her friend Willow, and usually when she woke up in the morning she had sheet creases in her cheek.

Maybe she could creep out of bed, make herself presentable and then get back in.

"Morning," Russell's low voice rumbled under her cheek.

She was curled around his body, her head resting on his chest. She had felt his arms around her all night, and that had been nice. Well, more than nice, she thought. She'd never slept as soundly with someone else in her bed.

"Morning," she said, not tipping her head up toward him. "I should go and get you some coffee."

"You should? Why?" he asked, stroking his hand up and down her bare arm.

"Don't you want one?" she asked, realizing she was out of practice in waking up with a man.

"I do, but I will make you a cup. I didn't get much of a tour last night, but I think I can find the kitchen."

"Okay," she said.

He tipped her head back and she stared up into his light eyes. They were becoming so familiar to her, so dear to her, and she knew that if nothing worked out between them, she'd always cherish this memory. He leaned down and kissed her. His mouth moved slowly over hers, until her eyes drifted closed and all the fears that had been circling around in her head disappeared.

His hands smoothed down her back and cupped her buttocks, drawing her into his body. "You feel good first thing in the morning."

He rubbed his beard-stubbled chin against the top of her head and hugged her closer. She sighed and let herself relax into him.

"That was a big sigh," he said.

"I know."

"What are you worrying about now?" he asked.

"Everything," she said, pretty sure that covered it all.

He laughed. "Damn, woman, you even wake up worrying?"

"Yes, I do," she admitted. "I wish I didn't, but that's the way I am."

"You need a man to lean on so you don't have to worry so much," he said quietly.

"I do," she admitted, looking up at him. She wanted to

believe he was that man. But she still wasn't one hundred percent sure, and she doubted she ever would be.

"What am I going to have to do to prove myself to you?" he asked.

She just shook her head. "I wish I knew. I keep waiting for this feeling inside of my stomach to settle down."

"That's excitement," he said. "You don't want that to go away."

But she did. She didn't like feeling as if she was caught up in a hurricane, and that was exactly what life with Russell was like. "I'm not sure."

"I know. Why don't I get you some coffee while you shower, and then we can share a cab to your office?"

"Why my office?" she asked.

"Because I am seeing you to work today, after giving you a proper morning with your lover," he said.

She knew it was silly, considering the age they lived in, but the word *lover* always gave her an illicit thrill. "Why do you put up with my doubts?"

"I have them too, and until they are abated for you, I know we aren't where we need to be in order to move forward."

She bit her lower lip and sat up next to him, bringing the sheets with her to keep covered. "What do you mean, 'move forward'?"

"I mean marriage," he said. "It's a bit hard for me to get my head around, but I can't see a future for you and me where we are simply live-in lovers. I know you want more and I think I do too."

"Think? Well, I'm not going to say yes to marrying you until you're sure you want it," she said. "People who feel trapped in relationships end up wrecking them."

He nodded. "I suspect that's why you're still worrying

about my level of commitment and I'm still not sure what it is."

"I think you're right," she said, feeling better about being with Russell than she had thought she would when she woke up this morning. "Ugh, I forgot about my hair. Is it crazy?"

"Yes," he said with a wicked grin. "But I love it. You look as if you've had a very enjoyable night."

She shook her head, reaching out to pinch him. "You were supposed to say no."

"Why would I? I assume you'll see yourself in the mirror. And to be honest, I like you this way. It's the real you without any of the barriers of makeup. It's just Gail Little, and I like her."

Those few words soothed away the last of her early-morning worries. She realized that Russell had a tendency to do that. He always found a way to say the right things to make her feel at ease, even in the oddest moments. "Thanks."

"Thank you for last night and for the last month. When I went to the matchmaker, I honestly believed I wasn't going to find anything different than I had experienced before. But you surprised me, beautiful."

"You've surprised me too."

"In a good way?" he asked, arching one eyebrow at her.

She studied him for a long minute. "Yes, I think so."

"Damned by faint praise," he said as he swung his legs to the side of her bed and stood up in all his glorious nakedness. "Maybe coffee will help win your heart."

She doubted coffee would help. "Stand there for a minute and maybe that will help."

"Like this," he said, putting his hands on his hips and turning to face her fully. She skimmed her gaze over his muscled form and could only nod.

He was a very good-looking man, and this morning she felt very happy and lucky to call him hers.

Russell didn't really know what he was going to do with Gail. He knew the producers of the show wanted him to make some romantic gesture on their last date, and he wanted to fulfill his obligations to them, but a bigger part of him wanted to blow Gail's mind. Defy her expectations.

She'd entered into the show and the matchmaking with the expectation that she'd find a man who'd marry her. But he knew he wasn't the guy she wanted to spend the rest of her life with...or at least he hadn't been in the beginning. And to be fair, he'd gotten what he wanted from Gail when Malcolm had agreed to sell his shares to him. But Russell still wasn't ready to walk away from her.

He'd meant what he'd said to her earlier. He couldn't see them simply living together. He needed to know she was bound to him, and that nothing from his past was going to come between them and take her away from him.

He heard the shower stop and realized he hadn't finished making the coffee. Gail made him question things that he'd always taken for granted. Take this morning—he had never had to assuage a woman's worries after a night with him. But she was different. With each day they were together, he was learning more and more about how different they were.

"Do you want to get a shower?" she asked from the doorway. She was wearing a summer suit and had her wet hair pulled back in a tight bun. She couldn't have looked more different from how she'd awakened in his bed if she'd suddenly shaved her head. She was all professional now, and he was still in his boxers.

"I guess I will. I'm afraid I never got the coffee made," he said.

"That's not a big deal. I'll take care of it while you're cleaning up."

There was awkwardness between them that he could tell she felt as well. They weren't close enough to be doing these intimate daily rituals, yet he wanted them to be. He knew that only once they started waking up together every morning would he really get a feel for what was coming between them.

"Have you ever lived with a man before?" he asked her.

"No, I haven't. I'm… There just hasn't been anyone who I wanted to spend all my time with."

"For me as well," he said. "Though I have had women live in my houses, it never felt like this does."

She gave him a very shy smile. "Is that good?"

"Yes, it is," he said, noticing she wore the chocolate-pearl-and-diamond earrings he'd given her. Some of his own doubts disappeared. He knew himself well enough to know that he was going to make Gail his completely. Now that he'd acknowledged he couldn't be happy with anything less than marriage, he was going to do everything in his power to make that happen for them.

"I don't need coffee," he said.

"Well, I do," she admitted. "I'm a wreck until I have at least one cup."

"Then I'll leave you to it. I'm going to bring over some stuff so that, when I spend the night here from now on, I'll be able to shave."

"Don't you think you should ask?"

He closed the gap between them and put his hands on her hips to draw her in close to his body, forcing her to tip her head back and look up at him. "No. You like to be difficult."

"I do," she admitted with a grin. "I think everyone has made your life too easy up until you met me."

He pinched her ass and then leaned down to give her a long, deep kiss. His erection stirred again, and he swept her up in his arms and carried her back to the bedroom.

"I just got dressed," she said.

"Would you like me to stop?" he asked, tracing his finger over the lines of her face as he set her on her feet. She had delicate features, but usually she acted like such a powerhouse that he didn't notice it until they were alone like this.

"No, I was just being silly."

"Good," he said. "I wanted to make love to you as soon as we woke this morning, but you seemed to want to get out of bed."

"I was unsure what to do," she said. "It's been a while since a man slept over."

"I'm glad. I don't like the thought of sharing you with anyone else. Even a memory."

She looked up with a quiet stillness that he knew meant utter sincerity from her. "There is no other man that can compare to you."

His ego and his erection grew at those words. He pushed her back on the bed and came down next to her, cradling her in his arms. Telling her with his caresses just how much she meant to him.

He slowly undressed her and saw that she had another fabulously sexy matching bra-and-panty set. He vowed that he'd unlock that latent sensuality that she kept hidden beneath conservative suits and tidy hair. He wanted her wild and aching for him.

And he set about arousing her until she was begging him to take her. He pulled her over his lap so she could ride him, with her thick hair falling around them in a veil and her pretty breasts bouncing with each gyration of her hips. He leaned up and suckled one nipple and felt her tighten around him. He jerked his hips forward, jetting his completion and calling her name.

When they were both spent, she fell forward in his arms, resting her head in the crook of his neck. He held her tighter than he intended and knew deep in his soul, he wasn't letting her go.

Gail showered with Russell and then they got dressed together. She tried not to let the feeling of joy that was swamping her right at the moment get to her, but it was hard not to. Russell had turned out to be absolutely perfect for her in a way that she'd never expected.

On the elevator ride down in her building, she hugged his arm to her and smiled up at him.

"What was that for?" he asked.

"Just because," she said, not ready to admit to him what she was just acknowledging to herself. She loved him. It was overwhelming, and when she looked at him, the truth just stared back. He might be a billionaire jet-setter, but he was also the man who had won her over with his honesty and his charm.

He squeezed her back. "We're good?"

"Very good," she admitted. Finally admitting how she felt about him put to bed all the doubts that she couldn't figure out. It was as if worrying over Russell had just been a way to mask what she really felt.

They reached the lobby, where Russell gestured for her to walk in front of him and she did. Turning back to smile at him as the doorman opened the lobby doors to the street, she stumbled, and Russell reached for her arm to steady her.

As flashbulbs exploded around them.

A cacophony of words barraged them, as cameras, microphones and paparazzi surrounded them. She couldn't understand a word they were saying as Russell wrapped his arm around her, guiding her to his waiting car. His driver had the backseat door open, and Russell hustled her into the car. The door closed solidly behind them, and there was an almost unnatural silence in the interior.

"What was that about?" she asked, feeling dazed and a little scared.

"I'm going to find out now. I'm sorry, Gail, but I need to go to my office."

"That's okay. You can drop me off at mine," she said.

"I wanted this morning to be about you," he said.

"It's fine," she said, but she knew that it wasn't. While they'd been alone in her apartment, it had been easy for her to pretend that they were meant to be together. But this was the first time in her life that she'd been surrounded by a swarm of photographers, and she knew that was a normal occurrence in Russell's life. She hadn't considered that. She'd been living in a little bubble of her own making, and it was time for her to be serious about her emotions.

Loving Russell wasn't a neatly tied package, and she was coming to realize that it actually brought about more complications than she would have guessed. He was on his phone, and she didn't even pretend that she wasn't listening to his conversation.

"They were outside of her apartment, Dylan. I want to know who gave them Gail's information," Russell said.

He was angry. His body was tense and his free hand clenched in a fist. Gail had the first inkling that she really was important to Russell. That helped her calm down. He had been right earlier when he'd said that she needed someone—well, him—to take care of the things she worried about.

And her earlier fears about hair and morning breath

seemed so inconsequential compared to this. She should have been worried about their lifestyles, as she had been in the beginning. But Russell had done such a good job of wooing her and making her forget how different they really were.

She felt the sting of tears behind her eyelids and turned away, fumbling for her sunglasses. It didn't matter how the information about her had gotten out in public. Now that she'd seen that swarm, she knew that, despite her feelings for Russell, she couldn't live like that. She never wanted to be in that situation again.

"You okay?" he asked.

"No," she said. "I'm sorry, Russell, but I can't handle this."

"It's fine. I'm going to find out who leaked your address and we'll take care of that. They won't bother you again."

"I don't think you can control it."

"Hell. I will do what I can to make sure you feel safe. I think it might be best if you move into my place for the time being, and I will hire a bodyguard to travel with you."

She shook her head.

"They will not be as bad from now on," he said.

"It doesn't matter. I can't do this, Russell. That's what I'm trying to say to you. Keep the bodyguard and all of your threats for the paparazzi. I'm not going to be part of your life anymore."

"You can't decide that unilaterally," he said. "We are in a relationship and both have a say in what happens."

"I know. It's just that today I realized, no matter how you are with me in private, I'm always going to be dealing with your past, and I'm just not up to that, Russell. I want to be. I wanted my feelings for you to make everything okay, but they won't—they can't."

"Coward," he said. "You are bailing based on the

chance that you might be hurt, without seeing that you are running away again. Hiding behind those barriers you have put in place to keep yourself safe. But you can't see that you are withering behind those walls, Gail."

"You might be right. I'm afraid and I thought that maybe... It doesn't matter. The truth is I'm not really the right woman for you, and you're not the right man for me. I want quiet time with you and being able to be in public without being followed, or worrying that something from your past is going to spring up to interfere with our lives again."

Russell ran his hand through his hair. "Penny is going to be taken care of, and that threat will be gone. There's nothing in my life to warrant attention, not going forward, not with you."

She shook her head. "I can't. The driver can just let me out here," she said, realizing they were circling the block where her office was.

Russell signaled the driver to stop. "I never figured you for someone who'd run away."

"It's funny, I've always known that I would."

She opened the door and got out, closing the door and walking away without looking back. She didn't even realize she was crying until she was in the elevator on the way up to her office. She knew she wasn't just mourning her short-lived love and happiness with Russell, but also the death of the dreams she'd secretly harbored for her entire life.

Fourteen

The hotel was bustling with activity when he entered the lobby. The doorman greeted him and people waved and smiled, but Russell wasn't in the mood to keep up the image of the good-natured owner today. He was ready to explode and didn't know what pissed him off more. The fact that Gail had walked out over something so ridiculous, or the fact that he'd let her.

He was tired of dealing with the mess that Penny had stirred up. It was time to put an end to it. He'd done what he could to help her out, and in the past he would have let things ride, but he wasn't about to let Gail back out of the relationship they'd been building.

He walked into his office to see Dylan on his phone, Mitsy on her phone and two lawyers waiting in the guest chairs. He signaled the lawyers to enter his office and came to a halt when he realized that he needed to know the exact details of what was out there in the press. He wanted to fight it, but he had to know what he was up against.

"Do you know what's going on? Why were there photographers at my girlfriend's apartment this morning?" he asked Jack Monroe, his lead attorney.

"Near as we can tell, Penny's filed a palimony suit against you, alleging that you won't acknowledge her or her child. She has named Gail Little as the 'other' woman."

This was worse than he had thought. "What are the options? I want her stopped and this to end."

"We can take care of it, but it's not going to be pretty, and Ms. Thomson will understand that you will never give her anything."

"Do it. She might cost me a merger as well as Gail. I want her stopped, and I don't want to have to deal with anything like this again."

"Understood. We will file the papers necessary to stop her."

"Good. I don't want to hear from you until you have results," Russell said, then realized how abrupt he was being. "It's not your fault. Sorry if that came out wrong."

"Not a problem," Jack said. "We are used to dealing with stressful situations."

"Thanks," he said.

The two men left, and Russell wasn't alone for a minute before Mitsy walked in. She was dressed in a sunny spring suit that made her seem cheery. Knowing his assistant as he did, he suspected she'd dressed that way because of what was going on today.

"What's up?" he asked her.

"Malcolm is on the line and he's not happy," Mitsy said. "I've been as placating as I could be, but he won't listen to me."

Russell nodded and then smiled reassuringly at his assistant. "Thanks for doing what you could. I'll talk to him now. I need a bouquet of wild flowers sent to Gail. I will email you the message I want on the card."

"Yes, sir. Anything else?"

"Probably, but for now I'm good," he said.

She left, quietly closing the door behind her, and he walked over to his desk and picked up the phone. He stared at the blinking light where the call waited and tried to get his feelings for Gail out of the way so he could simply be a businessman again. He could do this. He'd wined and dined this man and made him see the world from Russell's perspective. All he had to do was somehow convince him that this latest blowup with Penny was just water under the bridge.

"Holloway," he said, unable to keep his lack of patience out of his voice. After all he'd done to assure Malcolm he was a changed man, Russell found himself right back where he'd been six months ago, when Malcolm had first refused to sell to him.

"Damn, boy, you know how to rile up the women, don't you?" Malcolm asked. "First, Ashley and I want to make sure that Gail is okay."

Gail wasn't okay and frankly, Russell had a better idea of how to finesse Malcolm than he did how to win Gail back. There was no way she was going to believe that his past wasn't going to pop up from time to time, and Russell knew very well he couldn't control how someone else acted.

"She's fine. I'm hiring a bodyguard to keep the paparazzi away from her."

"Good thinking," Malcolm said. "I assume that the stuff we are hearing about you is all untrue?"

"First of all, the child isn't mine, Malcolm, which is something that I've told Gail. I am not abandoning the baby or its mother," Russell said. "We were through long before I met Gail."

"I'm going to need more information than that or the deal is off," Malcolm said.

Russell thought about it long and hard. He really didn't have time to explain himself to Malcolm. He should be at Gail's office forcing her to talk to him, but this was business.

Malcolm said something else, but Russell had stopped listening. Business. He was going to end up all alone if he kept giving priority to things like this. Yes, he wanted to move into a new market segment, and his board had demanded it, but he needed to get his personal life in order first.

"Malcolm—sorry, mate, but I've got to go to Gail. This entire thing is a mess, and I can't leave her alone."

"Hell, boy, I think you might have really changed for this woman. We can talk later," Malcolm said, hanging up the phone.

Russell walked out of his office. "Forget the flowers, Mitsy, I'm going over there myself. Dylan, hold down the fort until I get back. The only one I need to talk to is my attorney. I'm not available to anyone else."

"Yes, sir," Mitsy said.

"I've never been in charge before," Dylan said.

"You've done it a thousand times, just not by yourself. You have my confidence, and I'm sure you can handle anything," Russell said.

He walked out feeling like a new man. This crisis had put in perspective for him what was really important. It wasn't a new market in the hotel industry. It wasn't his reputation as a jet-setter. It was one woman who didn't give a crap about any of that.

One woman who'd made him realize that being with

her was all he really needed, and he hoped he hadn't left it until too late to tell her and convince her that he needed her.

Gail couldn't really be upset or blame anyone else for what had happened this morning. It was just that she'd been focusing on Russell and thinking if she was able to trust him, then she'd get what she wanted from the matchmaking. But all of a sudden, none of that mattered. The truth was that they were just too different, and no amount of dating or assurances from Russell was going to change that.

She'd spent her entire life in PR but had never really known until today that you couldn't change perceptions. Not really. There was always going to be one little thing from the past that would continuously come up and make a mockery of whatever new life you thought you'd built.

Truth was, she just wasn't meant for a husband and a family. She saw that now. She'd have to trust another person—a man—with every part of her being. If she couldn't trust Russell, whom she really did love, then perhaps she just wasn't wired to trust anyone.

Her assistant, J.J., was sitting at his desk when she walked in. "You are on the ticker. I mean big-time. Several of our clients have sent sympathetic emails, and one of them volunteered to punch any photographers who bother you."

"Thanks," Gail said. She felt wounded and wasn't truly sure what to do next. This was out of her realm of what was acceptable.

J.J. stood up and came over to hug her. "What can I do?"

"I don't know," she said, then shook her head and forced herself to stop feeling everything. She'd deal with this.

This was what she'd made a career of. "Actually, a cup of tea would be great, and then I have to make some calls. I need you to deal with anyone new today. I'm not talking to the press, and I have no comment on anything involving Russell Holloway."

J.J. nodded. "I can handle that. In fact, if you want to go home…"

"I can't. They know where I live," Gail said. That hurt a lot because her apartment had been a sanctuary for so long. She'd made it into the perfect little homey place where she went to dream, and now those dreams were sullied.

"Okay. I have a friend with a place on Long Island—I can call him if you'd like," J.J. offered.

"Thanks. Let me see what I can come up with first," Gail said, realizing she didn't want anyone to know where she went. Maybe she'd head to her grandmother's house in Florida, where she wouldn't have good internet reception, and her grandparents would make her fattening food and just love her. And the quiet of the swamp could soothe the feelings of heartbreak that were sweeping through her.

She knew she couldn't blame Russell. From the beginning, she'd tried to keep herself from falling for him. But how could she not, when he had so many of the qualities that she'd always secretly wanted in a man. She knew now that she'd been destined to fall for him from the beginning.

Her iPhone rang, and she glanced down to see Russell's picture on her screen. It was the photo of the two of them she'd had Kat take that day on the yacht. She hit Ignore and turned her chair away from her desk to stare out the window at the building next to hers. It was all brick on this side, and she just stared at that wall, hoping that somehow she'd easily fall out of love with him. That somehow she'd figure out how to bow out of a show that her friend was producing, and that by some weird miracle, she'd be able to continue her business without ever having to talk to anyone again.

She shook her head. She was being melodramatic. But she was just going to allow herself these few minutes of being a little down, and then she'd figure out a plan.

She pulled out her Clairefontaine notebook and ran her hand over the smooth paper. She liked the blank page, because she knew she had infinite possibilities of where her plan could take her. She picked up her fountain pen and decided to treat herself as she would a new client.

She'd advise her client to get out of the spotlight. So she jotted that down. She'd advise her client to try to ensure she was never in that situation again. She put that down next, and then couldn't help but add get rid of the negative influence. That got a frowny face next to it.

She wasn't sure she wanted to get rid of Russell.

She closed her eyes and remembered this morning when she'd realized that she loved him. Just because she'd only now acknowledged the feelings didn't mean they weren't strong and very real. God, she wasn't sure she was going to be able to get over him.

A part of her didn't want to. She wanted to have Russell in her memory—no she didn't. She wanted him in her life. She wanted him to be the guy she'd come to know, and not a man who was ruled by past girlfriends and media crises.

She drew a line across the page and started on a different plan. A plan that would fix Russell's troubled past once and for all. A plan that would give her what she wanted from him.

She wasn't sure where to start, but the ex-girlfriend seemed the best place. She wondered how much of this was maliciousness and how much of it was simply a broken heart. If she was honest, she had no idea what type of person Penny Thomson was. It was funny to her that someone she'd never met could have so much influence over her own life.

She'd go and visit Penny, she thought. But before she could even do a Google search for her address, her office door opened and Russell stood there.

Russell walked into Gail's office. He had made her a promise, back in the beginning when they'd met, that he was in this relationship to win. And he wanted them both to be winners. He wanted to have her by his side when he faced down trouble from his past or triumphs in the future.

Being on the phone with Malcolm had solidified everything for him. He wanted this woman, not just in his bed and in his arms at night, but also in his life. Episodes like this morning's wouldn't have happened if he hadn't been hesitating to make her his, really make her his.

"What are you doing here?" she demanded.

"We kind of weren't done talking earlier," he said.

"I was. There isn't anything else to really say," she said.

"There's a lot more. You didn't give me a chance to tell you how foolish I thought you were being to run away."

She tipped her head to the side and shook it. "I seem to recall you mentioning that."

"I did, didn't I? But that wasn't what I really meant."

"What did you mean?"

He stepped into her office and closed the door behind him. He took a deep breath and realized that this was the most vulnerable he'd been since his parents had been killed in that fiery car crash.

"I don't want you to walk away from me," he said. "I can't live without you."

"You can't live without me, or you can't grow your business without me?" she asked.

"I couldn't care less about my business right now. I cut Malcolm off and told him I had to make things right with you before I could even consider his issues with my reputation."

"But you talked to him?"

"Don't. Stop trying to twist everything around so I'm the bad guy. I'm not," he said, and as his focus narrowed to just Gail, he knew what he had to do. What he had to say. And that knowledge only came with the soul-deep certainty that she was the woman he'd been waiting for his entire life.

"I love you," he said. The words just came out without any real planning.

Her eyes widened and she shook her head again. "You don't. Just a few hours ago—"

"A few hours ago I was trying to figure out how to spend more time with you. For the first time in my adult life, getting to the office was the last thing I wanted to do. I don't care about new deals and making more money if I don't have you by my side. You make it all worthwhile."

"I do?" she asked.

"Yes, you do," he said, walking around her desk and spinning her chair to face him. He drew her to her feet and into his arms.

"I don't know.… I'm afraid to believe it. Just this morning I realized how much you meant to me.… I love you, too, Russell."

He kissed her with all the passion and determination in him. He'd been so afraid that his inexperience with love would make him say or do the wrong thing. But this was Gail, and he was coming to realize that he knew her best.

She wrapped her arms around his waist and rested her head against his chest. "I've been busy thinking of what I needed to do. I was going to fix your problem with Penny."

Russell lifted her up and sat down in her chair, then settled her on his lap. "Making a list?"

"Of course, that's the way I operate. I did just sit here and feel sorry for myself for a little bit. But then I figured I had to do something or I'd go nuts," she said.

He pulled the pad of paper toward him and saw her first list. "I'm sorry."

"Sorry?" she asked, looking up.

"Yes, I haven't been completely honest with you," he said.

He saw all the color leave her face and knew that he hadn't come close to clearing all the hurdles he had to convince Gail that he was her Mr. Right.

"What else could there possibly be?" she asked.

And he tried to find the words. Well, of course, the actual words were easy, but he tried to think of a way to say them. A way to tell her that if she stayed with him she'd never have her dream family. But he couldn't skirt the truth any longer. He couldn't pretend to be something he wasn't. And if he'd learned anything from the entire fiasco with Penny, it was that secrets could definitely hurt his future.

"I'm sterile," he said, opting for simplicity. There really wasn't any other choice.

"Pardon?" she asked.

But he knew she'd heard him. She put one hand to her throat and then leaned her head forward.

"I know you want a family—"

"It's why I went to a matchmaker. My body is on a short clock. It won't be long before I won't be able to conceive.… Maybe fate is trying to tell me something."

"Adopt?" he said, throwing out the option he'd considered.

She gave him a sad sort of smile. "I think you might be

right. I can't fall out of love with you, Russell. God knows I've been trying to make that happen since I first realized you weren't the shallow playboy you seemed to be."

"Really?" he asked, afraid to believe it. "I know you can do better than me, but I promise you'll never find a man who loves you more."

She was so close that he could see the pretty colored rings of her iris and realized that her eyes weren't just brown, but had a lot of gold in them, too. He squeezed her closer, thankful that he'd found her. That the matchmaker had the good sense to listen, not only to what he'd said he wanted, but to truly understand what Russell had needed.

"And I'm sorry for this morning," he said.

"How could you have avoided that?" she asked.

"I should have taken you to my place, where I could have protected you better. We would have used the underground parking garage."

She shook her head. "They would have been waiting there. We can't put off the inevitable. I think you need to talk to Penny."

"I've already sent my attorneys to deal with her, and I can promise you that she won't be bothering us anymore. I'm moving on to a new life with you, Gail. And the problems of the past are going to stay there."

"Are you sure you want that?" she asked. "I'm never going to want to party every night. You've only had a glimpse of what I'm really like."

"We will take our time and get to know each other better. But I already know the most important thing of all."

"And that is…?"

"That I love you and you love me. Everything else will fall into place."

"Promise?" she asked.

He looked into her deep chocolate eyes and kissed her

for a long moment before lifting his head. "I promise. Do you believe me?"

She put her arms around his neck and leaned in close to whisper in his ear. "You are the only one who I would believe."

Russell laughed and hugged her even closer to him. Thankfully, he'd found the one woman in the world who could tame his bad reputation and claim his wild heart.

Epilogue

The last date for *Sexy and Single* arrived, and Gail was a little sad to know that it was ending. She and Russell were living together and working to figure out their future. Russell had closed the deal with Malcolm, who had been impressed when Russell had hung up on him and put his personal life in front of business.

Gail was impressed, too. She knew that Russell would always be dedicated to his business, but it was nice to know that when it mattered he put her first.

Penny had come clean about using Russell to try to manipulate the father of her baby into marrying her. But once she'd stopped trying so desperately to find a man to marry, she had realized she would be fine on her own. She was giddy with the anticipation of having her baby, and Gail was a bit jealous of the other woman, who had come to her house to apologize in person for being such a witch—Penny's words, not Gail's.

It was almost time for the date to begin. Gail went into the confessional after her hair and makeup were done and turned on the camera.

"This is my last date with Russell, and though it didn't go as I'd expected, I couldn't be happier with the results. Matchmaking might not be right for everyone," she said. "But it was for me."

She turned off the camera and was led down the hall to the same exhibit hall where they'd had their first meeting. Just reflecting back on it made her smile. She'd been so sure that the Kiwi playboy was Mr. Wrong then. But Russell had proved to be so much more than just a fictional made-up guy could ever have been.

She was directed to sit at the table set for dinner. There was a champagne stand next to the table with a bottle chilling in the ice. She glanced around the room and saw Willow, who waved at her, and the rest of the camera crew, but Russell wasn't here yet.

Then he entered wearing a white dinner jacket and black pants. His smile was a thousand watts when their eyes met, and he walked straight over to her.

"Action," Willow called.

Gail admitted to herself that the camera was one thing she wouldn't miss. Still, she smiled up at Russell as he walked to the table, and he arched one eyebrow at her. "I never thought that we'd get to this."

"Me either," she said, unable to control the joy that was bubbling up inside her. "I thought you were going to end my dreams for finding a husband."

"I guess that means I won," he said with a cocky grin.

"You might think so, but I believe we are both winners," she said.

"Not yet," he replied, getting down on one knee next to her chair.

He took her hand in his and dropped a kiss on the back of it.

"Gail Little, will you do me the honor of being my wife?" he asked.

"Yes!" she answered, wrapping her arms around his shoulders to hug him. He grabbed her around the waist and lifted her out of the chair, hugging her tightly. She tipped her head and he kissed her. In that embrace she felt all of her hopes for the future and all of his love tied together.

Slowly Russell lowered her to her feet and pulled a box from his pocket. He took a ring with a large marquise-cut diamond from the box and put it on her finger.

"I hate to admit it, but the matchmaker really knew her stuff when it came to you and me," Russell said.

"I agree."

They sat down to eat dinner and Gail didn't let go of Russell's hand the entire time. When Willow finally called cut and production wrapped, Gail breathed a sigh of relief. Doing a TV show wasn't her thing.

"You look relieved," Willow said, coming up to her after the microphone had been removed. Russell was a few feet away having the same thing done to him.

"I am. It's not that I regret doing this, because I wouldn't have met Russell without it, but I am so glad it's over," Gail said.

"I can tell. Thanks," Willow said.

"For what?" Gail asked her friend.

"For letting me take your matchmaking idea and turn it into a TV show."

"Did I have a choice?" Gail asked with a cheeky grin. She couldn't help smiling, because she was simply happy with her life.

"No," Willow said with a laugh. "I never thought it would really work. I mean I've been surprised by things before, but a matchmaker? I didn't think you and Russell were suited at all."

Gail agreed. "Russell says that we fill in the missing pieces in each other."

"Aw, isn't that sweet. You complete each other," Nichole said with a tinge of sarcasm as she joined them.

"We do. I don't care if it sounds a bit hokey."

Nichole nodded. "I agree. That was just jealousy on my part."

"Jealousy! From you? The hottest dater in the tristate area?" Gail asked. "Trouble in noncommittal paradise?"

"No," Nichole said. "Just envy. I sometimes wish I had a permanent guy in my life."

Six months ago Gail would have felt the same, but today luckily she had found a man who would make her happy for the rest of her life. That didn't mean that the relationship with Russell wasn't without its ups and downs.

Russell waved at her from across the room and Gail smiled at him.

"Earth to Gail," Nichole said, waving her hand in front of Gail's face.

"I'm here. I was just…"

"Daydreaming about your fiancé," Willow said. "I'm so happy for you."

"Me, too," Gail said.

Russell walked over to her and the other women moved off. But Gail didn't pay any attention to them. "What were you talking about?"

"You," she said.

"Good. I was talking about you. I called my mates back home and told them that I had finally found a girl to love."

"You told them that?"

"You betcha. I am not afraid to tell the world how I feel

about you, beautiful. You've given me more happiness than I'm sure I deserve."

She smiled up at him. "You've done the same for me."

* * * * *

PASSION

COMING NEXT MONTH
AVAILABLE JUNE 12, 2012

Harlequin® *Blaze*™
red-hot reads

Fall under the spell of fan-favorite author

Leslie Kelly

Workaholic Mimi Burdette thinks she's satisfied dating the
handsome man her father has picked out for her. But when sexy
firefighter Xander McKinley moves into her apartment building,
Mimi finds herself becoming…distracted. When Mimi opens a
fortune cookie predicting who will be the man of her dreams,
then starts having erotic dreams, she never imagines Xander
is having the same dreams! Until they come together
and bring those dreams to life.

Blazing
Midsummer Nights

The magic begins June 2012

Saddle up with Harlequin® series books this summer
and find a cowboy for every mood!

Available wherever books are sold.

www.Harlequin.com

HB79693

USA TODAY *bestselling author Kathie DeNosky presents the first book in her brand-new miniseries,* THE GOOD, THE BAD AND THE TEXAN.

HIS MARRIAGE TO REMEMBER

Available June 2012 from Harlequin® Desire!

Brianna wasn't sure Sam would want her here. After all, they were just one signature away from a divorce. But until the dissolution of their marriage was final, they were still legally married, which meant she was needed here.

As she turned to go through the hospital's Intensive Care Unit doors to Sam's room, Brianna bit her lower lip to keep it from trembling. Even though she and Sam were ending their relationship, the very last thing she wanted was to see him harmed.

"Does your head hurt, Sam?" she asked.

He reached for her hand. "Don't worry, sweetheart. I'm going to be just fine. If you'll get my clothes, I'll get dressed and we can go home. Hell, I'll even let you play nurse."

Why was Sam insisting they go home together? She had moved out of the ranch house three months ago. His obvious lack of memory bothered her. She needed to speak to the doctor about it right away. "Try to get some rest. We'll deal with everything in the morning."

Sam didn't look happy, but he finally nodded. Then he pinned her with his piercing blue gaze. "Are you doing all right?"

Confused, she nodded. "I'm doing okay. Why do you ask?"

"You told me you were going to get one of those pregnancy tests at the drug store," Sam said, giving her hand a gentle squeeze. "Were we successful? Are you pregnant?"

A cold, sinking feeling settled in the pit of her stomach. He didn't remember. She had miscarried in her seventh week, and that had been almost six months ago. Something was definitely wrong.

"No, I'm not pregnant," she said. "Now, get some rest. I'll be in later to check on you."

"It's going to be hard to do without you beside me," he said, giving her a grin.

Some things never changed, she thought as she left to find the neurologist. The sun rose in the east. The ocean rushed to shore. And Sam Rafferty could make her knees weak with nothing more than his sexy-as-sin smile.

What will Brianna do if Sam never remembers the truth?

Find out in Kathie DeNosky's new novel
HIS MARRIAGE TO REMEMBER

Available June 2012 from Harlequin® Desire!

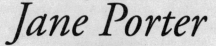

SPECIAL EDITION

Life, Love and Family

USA TODAY bestselling author

Marie Ferrarella

enchants readers in

ONCE UPON A MATCHMAKER

Micah Muldare's aunt is worried that her nephew is going to wind up alone in his old age...but this matchmaking mama has just the thing! When Micah finds himself accused of theft, defense lawyer Tracy Ryan agrees to help him as a favor to his aunt, but soon finds herself drawn to more than just his case. Will Micah open up his heart and realize Tracy is his match?

Available June 2012

Saddle up with Harlequin® series books this summer and find a cowboy for every mood!

Available wherever books are sold.

www.Harlequin.com

HSE65674